BONDED WITH MAGIC

DEEPTI GUPTA

COPYRIGHT
Unité Publication

Book Designed By: Rajvi Shah
Proof Reader: Rajvi Shah
Cover Design: Nikhil Jain

Any references to historical events, real people or real places are used fictitiously. Names, characters and places are products of the authors imagination.

Printed by Unité Publication, in India.
First printing edition 2022.
Unité Publication
Dhule, India.
414002

Unité Publication

Unité Publication whose name is derived from French word. It is a publication whose name itself means (Being Together), whose sole purpose of establishing it is to take everyone along.

The Unité Publication was established on February 2021. It is operated by Rajvi Shah and Nikhil Jain under which the publication of single books (solo) and collections (anthology, magazines) is being done efficiently by the highest and latest efforts tirelessly.

The Unité Publication doesn't give opportunities to just writers, poets, storytellers but also to photographers, chef, artist and many more. We publish recipe book, artistic book, photography book and many more.

Prior to the establishment of the community, we have ensured that our sole objective is to provide the highest platform to budding writers so that they can present their talents to world. The institution is moving towards promoting the activities of publishing at different levels.

You can connect with us for making your dream successful:

Contact Information,

Instagram:
@unite.publication_

Email:
unitepublicationrn@gmail.com

Contact Number:

+91 8208574289
+91 9624380410

DISCLAIMER

All the writings published in this book are originally written by the respective mentioned author, the Publisher has done their best to make them free from errors and plagiarism.

The mentioned characters or events in the book may be living or based on fiction but they neither depict any hate for any people, caste, religion or system nor they are meant to hurt anyone's feelings against anything.

Publisher would not be responsible, if in case the content is plagiarised. The respective author will be entirely responsible for the misbehavior.

ACKNOWLEDGEMENT

To have an idea, you need a creative mind and to initiate that idea, you need a backbone. Behind this solo book also, author had an idea, which gave author a space not only to write, also to describe her feelings and to publish it with some creative story. To initiate this idea, we had with us the team of **Unité Publication**. Thanks to the team for their support, their cover designing and allowing us to initiate our idea.

A special thanks to **Rajvi Shah and Nikhil Jain** the founder of the **Unité Publication** for giving us this opportunity through this project and making it successful in a short period with their energetic and active team without whom this project would not have been possible.

ABOUT THE BOOK

Bonded With Magic is a beautiful love story that took place in an fantasy magical world.
The romance among the characters will make you fall in love.

True love is destined and finds you by itself, no matter whether you were mind-washed in rage of revenge. Same goes with Marcus, he kidnapped Olivia to take revenge and the situation came when his heart started melting for her. The orphan Olivia was never aware of her royal inheritance and the moment her family found her Olivia's life became more of an mission. Olivia experienced Stockholm syndrome and fell in love with her kidnapper. Soon, both the hearts got bonded. After much of the drama, the magical kingdoms reunited and won over the Cruel Draco. Marcus and Olivia confessed and found their soulmates in each other and lived happily ever after.

One must give it a read to find out other interesting elements.

INDEX

LIST OF CHAPTERS

ABOUT THE AUTHOR

DEEPTI GUPTA

Deepti Gupta is an signed digital writer and an passionate poetess. She has her Master's degree in Finance. She is zealous to put her thoughts in words and love to share them with the world through her poems and novels. She is been writing since long but her work remained hidden in her diaries. One day when one of her friend got to read her poems he emphasized her to publish those. This is how her writing journey started. After that she never look back and keep on publishing her work as co-author with many National and International Anthologies.

She wrote many E-novels and covered genres such as romance, fiction, murder mystery, suspense and thrillers. Her E - novel "MET TO MEND" won the Young Adult Fiction Award on Starywriting(International E-novel portal)

She owns a youtube poetry channel by the 'Penning your emotions'.

Instagram@deepti_heartypoems
Facebook@deeptidilsediltak

PROLOGUE

Living a double standard of life is always challenging for wizards, and it becomes even more difficult when half of the magical world has already been destroyed by the evil dragons and the leftover Kingdoms were living under the sword of getting conquered. In this deadly situation, Marcus and Arthur who were also the victims of the attack survived since the age of 10. Their father, King Richard was declared dead when people saw him falling down the abyss and didn't return even after 15 years and their mother, Queen Vincent slipped into a state of coma after her encounter with the strongest killing spell enchanted on her by the cruel evil wizard king.

Both, the twin princes somehow grew up got educated both ways i.e **wizardry edu**cation and the muggles way of education.

MARCUS, the **elder twin turned** out to be the famous, rude and ruthless business tycoon of the country whereas ARTHUR, his only 5 minutes younger brother grew up as a kind and humble Doctor, who always indulge in charity events.

One and the only common thing in both is that they want to take revenge from the murderer of their father.

Unfortunately, No one was there to answer their numerous questions about who in actual attacked their kingdom and killed their father. They were desperately waiting for their mother to come out of the coma as soon as possible.

Jacob a betrayer minister grew them and took proper care of them, manipulative the children innocent minds to attack according to him. He sparks the flame of revenge in their hearts. Marcus blindly trusts Jacob and he also helps him in business.

On the other hand, Arthur never was able to trust Jacob. He finds him suspicious all the time that is why Jacob also maintained a distance from him.

14

CHAPTER-1 "SUGAR CANDY"

A beautiful young girl lay unconscious on the marble floor of a luxurious room.

The capacious room is all lushing with classy velvet curtains covering floor to ceiling windows, a king-size bed in the middle of the room, a big velvet sofa, incredible paintings hanging on the walls, expensive chandeliers and lamps strewing the magical light making the room look more lavishing, attached glass bathroom with jacuzzi is perfect for an astonishing bath. This room was so amazing and has all the opulrnce that everyone would love to stay here.

Suddenly, the door opens, and a tall, handsome man appears on the door.

"Finally, I found her. I found the source to take my revenge."

"Finally!" Marcus said to himself after he got informed by his guards that they caught the girl, he was looking for a long. He swiftly paced to the room where she was captivated. He pushed the door open and a smile crept over his lips by looking at the girl helplessly lying on the floor.

He may sound creepy but how can anyone expect him to be merciful towards the daughter of his father's killer. He menacingly paced towards her.

Unbelievably, out of his expectations. The girl looks alluring, her snow-colored skin, long red hair, pink lips and perfectly curved body is perfect to seduce any man.

He sheepishly thought in his head. He moved in and sat on the velvety couch with one hand supporting his head, looking at the innocent face of the sexy girl.

He impatiently waited for a few moments and when he lost control over his patience, he gestured to the jug of water that was lying on the centre table using his wizardry powers. The jug started flying in the air. Then, the water from the jug splashed on the girl's face, jug fell on the ground, scattered in pieces, a loud sound of glass smashing on the floor echoed in the room.

Even after all this, the girl did not move at all, and her reaction less body worsens his anger. He angrily stood up and walked towards the girl. He rolled his index finger on her face pushing the wet strands of hair away from her face. To his extreme surprise, his cold fingers touched her slightly warm skin and a sharp wave went down his spine.

He was all shocked at the same time and perplexedly rolled his eyes all over her. Her wet slender body was breathtaking, the black shimmered dress is now almost transparent, her cleavage is exhibited beautifully under the V neck of the dress, her willowy white legs are infuriating his manly desires.

He took her in his arms and put her on the king-sized bed. He forgets to blink staring at her. He was all lost in her beauty and perplexedly leaned on her, touched her lips with his index finger and that touch paced up his urges to get the revenge and suddenly a sharp spark rushing down his spine with another touch. He has never experienced this before.

"So Awful!"

He murmured in astonishment and was about to move away from her.

"Water, Water..."

She faintly murmured and rolled her tongue over her dry lips.

Her seductive voice turned him on, sending butterflies to his stomach. He furiously jumped out of the bed, picked out a small bottle of liquid from the bedside drawer and leaned over the girl's body, tossed the lid of the bottle, and put some drops on her dry lips with a creepy thought that just blew up in his head.

He is not a professional kidnapper or a criminal but he evidently was preparing for this day from ages.

She subconsciously licked the drops to quench her thurst.

He then turned to her and lay down by her side, tapping his lap with his fingers in excitement, it seemed that he was excitedly waiting for a movie to start. He curled his lips when the body of the girl showed some reaction.

He was carefully watching all the movements of that girl's body.

A moan escaped out of her mouth.

Her moans started getting over his nerves.

She moaned again raising her waist, the girl was now ready according to his plan. The stimulations in her body gave him satisfaction.

He menacingly glances at her. Then, he strongly grabbed her in his arms, looking at her fainted face. He excitedly rolled his fingers on her trembling lips, she moaned again with his touch. Her hot breath fans his face.

"OO girl,"... He groaned

Her moans triggered him hard. He ripped off the piece of her cloth slowly.

"I never thought my revenge would be so beautiful," he whispered looking at her face.

He couldn't control his urges and started flirting between her lips with his fingertips. Infuriating every inch of her sensitivity.

With his touch, she slightly woke up and screamed.

"Who the hell are you?" her words are more like whimpers. He came out of his trance with her whimpers.

She is your enemy! His brain scowls at him.

He grabbed her from her neck in rage.

"Aaahhh,...leave me!"

Her words didn't affect him at all. She is getting a bit conscious, looks dizzy but the drug reaction was unbearable to her, he knows. He slowly caressed her soft cheeks with his knuckles. She is now subconscious and can feel his touch on her skin "No!" She whimpered. But, she moans again with his cold finger touching her soft spots. He groaned, gripping her tightly.

He turned and put her on her chest for a while just to soak her in and he felt a strange calmness. The calmness he longed for since eternity. He closed his eyes taking, her scent and his father's painful screams echoed in his head. He threw her away on the floor. She tried hard to open her eyes to look at him and struggled to shake her head to wake herself. She tried hard to get up. Before she could respond.

He furiously treads towards her and pinned her to the wall. He smirked looking at the beautiful face of the woman caged in front of him.

"SUGAR CANDY", He gave her a new name rolling his eyes all over her naked body.

"My... name... is Olivia." She hoarsely replied.

"OOOH! you have the audacity to cut my words." He devilishly said.

"Leave me!" she groggily yelled. "I will leave you but not so easily!" He exclaimed tightly clenching her wrists.

"What do you want?" she groaned and tried very hard to get out of his grip. He pushed her back to the wall, her back hitted hard on the wall and she grunted in pain. His heart slightly twitched with her grunts, but his brain keeps on reminding him of the motive behind his actions.

"THIS IS JUST THE START OF YOUR NIGHTMARE!" He yelled throwing her back on the bed and frustratedly walked out of the room.

CHAPTER-2 "TRY YOUR LUCK"

The next morning,

A maid came into the room with a tray of breakfast for Olivia. She put the tray on the side table and walked towards the floor-ceiling window and pushed back the curtains from the window.

Olivia woke up with the noise, her eyes were dazzled with the light, she involuntarily raised her hand to block her eyes.

"Good morning, Miss", the maid looked at Olivia and greeted her,

"Who are you?"

"Where am I?" She groggily asked with a heavy head.

"My head...aaahh..." She groaned holding her head and looked around.

She is feeling some sourness in her body and a tinge of stiffness in her body are another question of concern to her.

She couldn't understand the changes in her body, so she tried to recall what happened to her? She just remembers that she went to a store, and the shopkeeper offered her candy as it was her birthday. She chewed that candy and after that, she blacked out.

"May I help you, Miss?" the maid politely asked.

"No," she shouted.

Olivia looked at her body, shocked to see that she had no clothes on her. A wave of panic went down her spine and she started screaming like crazy.

"Who are you guys? Where are my clothes? Who took off my clothes? Which is this place?"

 She turns red with rage and attacks the maid with a pillow. The maid defended herself, "Miss please calm down". She tried her level best to calm down Olivia.

Olivia jumped out of the bed, took the metal vase from the shelf and threw it towards the maid. The maid bent down to save herself.

The vase stopped in front of Marcus's face, who entered the room on hearing her screams.

The vase turned back to Olivia with the gesture of his eyes like a rocket, she turned aside to save her and the vase banging in the glass window shattered glass around.

She closed her ears tightly in fear. She gave a flaming, robust glance to Marcus, who was standing at a distance with his arms close to his chest and nastily looking at her naked body with a smile and signalling the maid to get out of the room.

Olivia looked down at her naked body, hurriedly grabbed the bed sheet and wrapped the bed sheet around her in embarrassment.

He took a step forward to her.

"No, don't come to me, you rascal."

He ignored her words and continued moving towards her, she looked back down the broken window, there was a deep, dense abyss.

"If you didn't stop, I will jump out," she warned him with a trembling voice, tears started welling up in her eyes and she tried her best to push them back and a knot went down her throat looking at Marcus menacing towards her.

He paused, she again looked back down the valley with fear and turned back, her nose poked into his chest, her eyes widened and shocked to see him too close to her.

"Why didn't you jump?" he scornfully asked, clenching her waist.

She tried hard to push him back, but he stood like a giant rock,

 "Who are you, creep?" She growled, grinding her teeth, and tried to get out of his grip.

"Don't change the topic now." He snorted with a devilish smirk creeping on his lips.

"Why do you bother your body? I will make it easy for you, sugar candy." Saying that, he pushed her out of the window.

She started falling into the abyss, she screamed and tightly closed her eyes. She felt that she was going to die, then suddenly she felt her movement stop. She opened her eyes and saw that she was swinging in the air. She did not fell into the ditch, fascinated that she survived, she heaved a relaxed sigh,

With a second thought, her heart skipped a beat with panic. How is she swinging in the air without any support?

"Hey, Sugar candy," He waved to her from the broken window.

She looked at his vicious face,

"Who are you?" " How did you do this to me?" She yelled swinging in the air, faking a sturdy look.

He raised his fingers and tossed her in the air. She shouted because of the force, tears were rolling out of her eyes. She was swinging in the air like a kite. After a while she lost breath having a panic attack and she fainted hanging in the air.

He looked at her and pulled her back with a spell and put her on the bed.

"Poor Girl," he muttered leaning over her, looking at her faint face

 "Why didn't you ask for mercy?" he asked in astonishment looking at her red tomato-like face,

"I want you to beg me." "I will make your life hell!"

"You can't be so calm, wake up," he slapped her face and shouted angrily. He loses his temper when he recalls she is here for his revenge.

She slightly shook her head; his fingerprints were clearly visible on her white cheeks.

She murmured, "Who are you? you monster, monster leave me," her eyelids are trembling, her words are shaking in fear.

He slapped her again and grabbed her shoulders and shook her, "open your eyes!", he shouted at her,

She tried hard to open her eyes, but she couldn't...

"Oh, what do you think of yourself, you poor girl, this is just the start, You can't blackout so soon."

He jumped out of the bed, took a glass of water from the side table and sprinkled water on her face.

She blinked her eyes and gazed at him, she immediately sat up gasping and anxiously pulled her knees to her chest, tears streaming down her cheeks and her face turned white.

"Let me go. Why did you take me here?" she asked in a scared voice,

"I like your tone!" he smirked and sat close to her. A knot of fear went down her throat and her panicked heart started beating furiously.

Olivia saw his body getting close and close to her, she involuntarily tried to cover her body with the bed sheet. He snatched the bed sheet from her,

"You rogue," she screamed.

"Oh... really?" Marcus raised his lips tenderly,

"I will show you how a rogue behaves?"

Marcus removed his T-shirt and threw it away showing his solid defined, muscular physique. The man muscular body covered the girl's delicate body shamelessly, his warm breath spelt on her sensitive neckline, the unfamiliar male scent that escaped from his breath parcelled her entirely,

The man's lips did not waver when he kissed the trembling cherry lips.

She pushed him back with force and tried to get up.

"Rascal," she screamed.

He again slammed her back on the bed, clenched her hands above her head and kissed her desperately. He showed aggression and pulled towards her.

Evidently, he was also a virgin till last night, now the taste of women made him mad, he just wants her all the time.

"Please don't do this...hmm, please, let me go...hmm", Olivia shook her head desperately and toughly heaved out each word. However, her each word could only roll in her mouth. It seemed like a whisper, which constantly stimulated this man's sense of arousal.

Marcus held her cheek in one hand, and bit her lip as punishment, "You have to pay for his sin!" He accentuated

"Please leave me," she pleaded.

He looked at her constantly streaming tears, and the strange feeling in his heart grew stronger and stronger. He loosened his restraints, turned over and got up, "You are mine and you have to bear me willingly or unwillingly." He yelled and furiously walked out of the room.

CHAPTER-3 "ESCAPE"

He was coming out of the door and a hand-blocked his way.

"What are you doing, Marcus?" he turned to the voice of his twin brother Arthur.

He shamelessly looked into his eyes.

"Don't you know what it is?" he rudely asked gawking his brows at his younger brother.

"WHO IS THAT GIRL? Arthur yelled pointing his index fingers towards Olivia who was crying, lying on the bed.

Marcus immediately closed the door.

"That's my revenge! None of your business!" he shouted.

"It's not an act of revenge, have you gone mad? She is innocent, you cannot punish her for the sins of others." Arthur scowls.

"I want her to feel the pain the same way we lived our lives," Marcus ruthlessly replied.

Arthur wrapped his arm around Marcus's shoulder and tried to calm down his anger,

"Brother, I understand your feelings, I also want him to pay for his sins, but not like this. Send this girl back to her house, she is innocent, don't drag her into it."

"No!" Marcus dismayed shoving Arthur's hand from his shoulder.

"She is Olivia." He angrily pointed his finger towards the closed door,

"Daughter of King Cox, she must pay for the sins of her father, nobody can stop me from doing this, not even my brother." The fire of revenge was flaming in his eyes.

Arthur was about to say something, but he stopped him in the middle, "Stay out of it, brother and this is not a request or advice, take this as my first and last warning to you. I never want you to spy here again and from now onwards, you better skip walking this aisle."

Marcus blind in the rage of his revenge. Arthur tried his best to stop Marcus, but he was not even ready to listen. On the contrary he warned Arthur. "I also want to have revenge but not against humanity. Torturing some innocent girl for others' sin is not what we learnt from our parents. I need to do something to save Marcus from committing some serious crime." Arthur thought

Heaving a deep sigh, he left the corridor.

Inside the room, Olivia is lying on the bed like a corpse, her face looks not less than a zombie with bruises all over her body, her white skin turned pale, and she is starving.

A maid re-entered the room to help her, this time she did not rebel,

"Miss, May I help you clean yourself." The maid was also shocked to see the scratches and bruises on her body, the bruises on her body were telling the story of the humiliation,

She grabbed Olivia. supported her back, and gently took her to the bathroom, put her in a hot water jacuzzi, and with some herbs in the water to heal her body,

Olivia soaks into the hot bubble bath, her muscles begin to relax with the heat, her body's sourness fades away, she wants to soak herself deep more and more into the water and slide down into the tub of water, the maid promptly caught her, as Olivia was about to drown herself in that huge tub.

"Be careful miss,"

"I'm fine," Olivia replied.

After half an hour, the maid took her out of the water and wrapped her in the bathrobe,

She helped Olivia come out of the bathroom put her on the couch and placed her foot on a soft cushion,

"Miss please have something to eat," she said offering a tray of fruit and vegetable porridge to her,

Olivia refuses to eat it.

"Miss, I request you. You look very pale and tired, please eat something." She politely requested her.

"I said No! No! No!" Olivia shouted.

The maid got scared and thought that Olivia would attack her again, she still stood firmly there,

"Miss, I regret to say, if you don't eat, Master Marcus, will punish both of us."

Olivia trembled in fear, "Is he Marcus?" her words trembled,

"Yes, Miss, he is master Marcus."

"Master?? Why do you call that demon master?" she surprisingly asked.

"Miss, please have some porridge," she ignored Olivia's question and gave her a bowl of porridge,

The smell of food watered her mouth, she did not refuse this time and started eating slowly with a spoon,

She eats peacefully wondering what is happening to her. Marcus's words are echoing in her head, revenge, pay for his sins, whose sin he is talking about? Why will I pay for others' sins? she asked herself,

She wondered and could not understand why she was kidnapped, punished and imprisoned in a luxurious room.

She finished eating porridge, looking at her empty bowl the maid interrupts, "Miss, would you like to have more porridge?"

She looked down at the empty bowl and replied "No, I am done," the maid took the bowl from her, put it in the tray and went out of the room with the tray,

Olivia sighed as the maid walked out. Olivia was tired of pretending to be calm, but inside her head, she was trying to find a way to escape from here: She walked towards the door and pushed the door slightly, to her surprise the door was not locked.

She peeked out the door.

"No guards, unprofessional kidnappers," she said smiling.

She saw many criminal series. In those series there always had several guards at the door of a captive.

She smiled and ran along the wide corridor. She saw the stairs and immediately ran down hurriedly. The stairs ended in a huge hall of that mansion, she looked around with surprise, such a grand hall, there was the main entrance in front of her, she escaped, passed by a beautiful golden main gate, much to her amusement that there is no guard to protect a billionaire, "Is, he so strong or so stupid?" She thought that she succeeded in running away.

Thinking that she should run away, she did not look back and ran into a dense forest surrounded by trees and wild bushes. After running for a mile, she stopped, looking around gasping.

"Help... someone, please help me, I'm stuck here," she screamed for help, but no one is there, she ran to find the way again, she keeps on running, after running for several miles she leaned her back on a tree and slide down tiredly, gasping, her eyes landed on her injured barefoot. This reminded her that she forgets to put on a sleeper and runs out in a bathrobe only, tears streaming down her eyes.

She looked at the loud sun, and her vision blurred and she blackouted because of injuries, thrust and hunger.

CHAPTER-4 "SEVERELY INJURED"

After that, a black Porsche stopped near her and a well-built man in black came out of the car and took her away.

After passing through the woods, the car went back in the same direction and entered the Golden Gate. The driver stopped the car near the main gate of the mansion. The tall man in black came out of the car, holding Olivia in his arms and stepped into the mansion,

Marcus was standing on the first floor and seeing the man carrying Olivia in his arms, her face touching his chest and his hands clutching her chest and legs, Marcus's face turned red, with the snap of his fingers he reached the man and grabbed Olivia from his hand and carefully put her on the sofa.

"Master, the lady, is severely injured", The man said pointing at her legs. He is Tom the main guard of Marcus,

Marcus turned his eyes on to her, rolling his eyes on her he noticed her pale face, and she has scratches all over her body because of the thorns of the forest, blisters broke out of her sol, and the rocks badly injured her feet, she looks like a mess. His heartache looking at her injured body and blood all over her body.

"Call Arthur, inform him it's an emergency," he screamed at Tom,

Arthur is a qualified doctor and runs a charitable hospital down the valley and has a small emergency hospital in the basement of the villa. He has his own laboratory where they invent and produce effective and affordable medicines.

Tom called the basement and asked for Arthur.

After 5 minutes, a senior doctor in a white lab coat came out of the elevator with his assistant holding the first aid kit, both came to Marcus and bowed him with respect, "How can I help you, Master Marcus?" The doctor asked politely,

"Where is Arthur?" Marcus grinned his teeth.

"I regret to say, as it is Sunday Master Arthur has gone down to the valley charitable hospital to treat the poor." The assistant calmly replied,

"Shut up, don't waste time just treat her in the best possible way," Marcus ordered the doctor raising his hand towards Olivia who is lying faintly on the sofa, Marcus is not interested in listening to any excuses.

The assistant put the First Aid kit on the table and opened it, the doctor checked her heart rate with a stethoscope and then checked her blood pressure, the assistant started giving her the first aid, he picked the cotton gauge dipped in the antiseptic liquid and started cleaning her wounds. As, he touched the gauge on her skin,

"Aahhhh!" Marcus mumbled, "Be gentle to her, you idiot," Marcus flickered,

"Yes, Master," Assistant Lynn said politely glancing at his face,

Marcus' eyes were rolling with each move of the doctor's hand on Olivia's body, he is actually feeling her pain which is a weird feeling for him, he never felt such pain before, He tightly clenched his hands into a fist.

"Where did you find her?" "Who is she?" The senior doctor asked while injecting her injection.

"The security guard found her injured in the woods." Tom quickly answered looking at the angry face of Marcus,

"Master, please have a seat." Tom raised his hand towards the sofa, Marcus sat on the front sofa with his arms close to his chest, continuously staring at Olivia with a pained look.

The doctor took an hour to give her the first Aid. Her wounds are now properly cleaned and bandaged wrapped around her feet and arms, bruises marks were visible on her skin. The doctor was about to open her bathrobe.

"Stop," Marcus shouted and shoved his hand from her bathrobe belt,

 "What the hell are you doing to her?" Marcus anxiously asked.

"Master, I am just examining, if she has more wounds under her clothes," The doctor said,

"No, I already checked that!" he hoarsely exclaimed

"Okay, then it's fine, Master, she is severely injured, I regret to say, her wounds are intense and will take 3-4 days for her to stand back on her feet, and she has a hairline fracture on her right wrist. She needs proper care and rest. I am afraid that she might have an encounter with a wild animal in the woods and fearfully she ran on the rocks barefoot.

She seems in a state of hysterical trauma. She actually needs 24/7 care. I injected her painkiller and a tetanus injection. She will be awake by morning." The doctor professionally explained.

"If you permit, I would like her to be under observation and want to shift her to the basement hospital." Marcus listened to him carefully and turned to look at Olivia. She is lying wrapped in bandages, like a half mummy, he felt pitiful,

"Whatever set up you need for her, you can have all that in the mansion, she will not shift anywhere," he uneasily said.

"As you say, master," The doctor nodded and bowed to him,

"Next time send a female doctor," Marcus wrathfully ordered the doctor who was about to leave,

The doctor gave a surprising look at Marcus. "I just asked for the dignity of a girl!" Marcus exclaimed.

"Sure master," The Doctor replied respectfully,

Lynn collected all the medical equipment, packed his first aid kit and both moved to the elevator,

Marcus took Olivia in his arms and teleported themselves to the bedroom.

He carefully put her on the bed, supported her fractured arm with a soft cushion, put a pillow under her head and covered her with a thin blanket, as it's a bit cold during the night at the cliff.

"How could she be so fragile?" he asked himself, glancing at her scratched face,

Arthur's words echoed in his head, she is innocent, right now looking at her he also felt like she is actually innocent as it's been two days, he has kidnapped her, but nobody came out to look for her, How can her family be so heartless with her?

He frowned and sat on a chair looking out of the window. The darkness of night clenched in his heart.

Now the luxurious room looks like an emergency ward of a hospital, which has all the medical equipment. Doctors did the setup, and the nurse was watching Olivia's recovery consistently, she also cleaned Olivia's body and put her on clean clothes.

In the middle of the night, Marcus was still sitting by the window looking at her in that position, the moon was in a string, and the light was enough for him to see her face clearly.

<u>CHAPTER-5 "HYPOCRITE"</u>

The moment she opened her eyes, he rushed over and stood by the bed.

"Sugar candy?" He looked down at her, still smiling with care and joy that had never been before.

Olivia stared blankly at him for a long time seemingly struggling to remember something.

"Oh? don't pretend you have memory loss?" he laughed.

"Welcome back."

"How can I forget a demon?" Olivia scoffed.

"Aoouch!" she groaned.

She pressed her fractured wrist while trying to sit,

He grabbed her softly from her shoulder and helped her sit, he kept two soft pillows behind her to support her back.

The nurse came forward to her and checked Olivia's heart rate and blood pressure, "She is fine now." The nurse said to Marcus,

He sighed and raised his hand, and the nurse left the room.

Olivia was shocked to see her injuries, when did she get so many wounds? She looked lost.

Marcus sits near to her and looking at her lost looks, he cleared his throat, "Ummhhdd."

"I must say you have so low IQ." He sneered.

"What?" she chuckled looking surprisingly at him,

"I mean the closet is full of comfortable clothes and the shoe rack has all the comfy shoes, you still chose to escape barefoot too in a bathrobe." he smiled raising the tip of his lip.

She lowered her head, she didn't realize all this before escaping,

"I was escaping from my kidnapper, not going out to participate in a marathon, that I would pick up comfy stuff to put on, I found an opportunity and I escaped," She said frustratedly.

"Oh really?" he said while arching his eyebrows,

"Do you really feel you got an opportunity to escape by luck"? he chortled.

She gave him a stern look her big black eyes were filled with anger,

"It is my territory, No one can even breathe here without my consent, and you thought, you got luck by chance opportunity." He laughed ironically.

"Monster!" she murmured.

He heard her words, "You are really an annoying girl, it was my meticulous plan to test your strength and smartness."

"Although, you are courageous that you ran all the way in the woods fearlessly and covered around 5 miles." he paused.

"However, I have no regret to say that your IQ is so low, he leaned over, and his male hormones spread over her face," she turned her head away.

"5 miles?" She thought how she ran for so long? She did not feel any pain from the injuries while she was running that she was so desperate to escape out of his reach, but to her bad luck he caught her again, tears dropped out of her eyes,

"Why am I here again? Who are you"? she asked with a saddened face.

He ignored her questions, A maid with the tray entered the room with the snap of his hand,

She put down the tray having two bowls of hot chicken soup on the table.

"Help her clean her mouth," Marcus ordered the maid gesturing his hand towards Olivia.

The maid nodded and went to the bathroom came out with a big glass bowl and a mouth wash and helped Olivia to rinse her mouth with the mouth wash, wiped her face with a damp warm towel.

He wanted her to have a clean mouth before eating something,

When the maid is done cleaning her. He gestured to the maid to leave, and the maid took the soiled towel, bowl and went out of the room, He took the bowl of hot chicken soup, tried the temperature, and put it in front of her, he smiled casually, "I will answer all questions, first you should eat something you look very pale, and you need to have enough strength to hear me."

Olivia lowered her head and chuckled, "What kind of revenge is this? First, you deliberately hurt me then now you are taking care of me faking affection."

She was starving and stretched out her left hand to carry the bowl, but her right hand was plastered,

"Aaahhh,", she groaned with pain and involuntarily supported her right arm with the left hand,

He looked at her pitiful eyes, took a spoon and sent it to her lips,

"I never thought that I would feed my enemies daughter like this," He frustratedly said: She widened her eyes and looked shocked to hear his daughter, "Do you know who my father is?" she anxiously asked.

He fed her another spoon and said, "of course yes, I know he is King Cox."

She coughed and spat some soup out of her mouth and a few drops spread over his hand.

"Shit..., you dirty girl," he growled.

He put the bowl on the side table handed her a tissue clean yourself and went to the bathroom to wash off his hand,

She was amazed to hear his words and couldn't understand what was going on?

She wanted to come out of the bed and removed the thin blanket from her legs and was shocked to see her banged feet, "What the hell happened to my legs?"

She screamed and tears burst out,

Marcus heard her scream and rushed out of the bathroom,

"Hey, why did you scream?" he asked cupping her face softly in his hands,

"My feet? What happened? I couldn't feel them," she cried in a louder voice poking her head in his chest, he clenched her tightly to his chest and his eyes sparkled with tears,

He wiped his tears and calmed her down, "Nothing happened there were some blisters and the foolish doctor wasted so much bandage on your feet, your wounds will heal soon till then, I am at your service, Sugar candy." He leaned her back to the cushion and took another bowl from the tray,

"Let me serve the princess." his voice is full of affection.

"Please tell me, who are you? Why are you doing this to me? I can't bear you; you are a hypocrite!" She pushed him back and kept crying,

Marcus dropped the bowl on the ground and stood from the bed, he was speechless hearing her words,

He walked out of the room, she kept yelling, "You are a demon, you ruined everything, you can't go away, answer me for god's sake please answer me... answer meeee."

He went out of the room angrily and slammed the door.

CHAPTER-6 "SHOCKED"

A nurse entered Olivia's room and tried to calm her down and injected her sedative so that she can sleep and rest. She is too weak and needs rest for faster recovery.

On the other side

Marcus entered his room writhing in anger, slammed the door and punched the wall so hard that his knuckles started bleeding. He leaned his forehead on the wall and a tear rolled out of his eyes and fell to the ground.

"It's good that you realised your mistake," Arthur taunted, sitting on the sofa sipping his coffee,

Marcus surprisingly looked back at him, "What do you mean, Arthur?" Marcus pretends to be calm.

Arthur put his coffee mug on the table and walked towards the cabinet, took out the first aid kit from the cabinet and moved towards Marcus. He grabbed his hand and cleaned the wound and applied an ointment on his hand,

"We are twins and don't forget that we can sense each other pains and sorrows, I mean, I never saw you crying for a girl," he said smirking.

"I was not crying." Arthur grinned his teeth,

"Oh really? Now you started lying to me as well, I just saw a demon all of the sudden change into a prince and trying to charm his princess." He snorted looking at the Marcus.

"Arthur, I am really not in a mood to get bullied by you, you better shut your mouth, you should go out and serve your poor patients, you are meant for them only!" he exclaimed frowning at Arthur.

"Marcus, why do you look so tired and frustrated, didn't you sleep last night?" Arthur taunted.

Marcus turned back to look in the mirror, Arthur is right his eyes are red and puffed, his face is actually looking tired. He thought looking into the mirror.

"Brother let's have a good breakfast and if you want you can admit your feelings to me, I will keep them secretive," Arthur said wrapping his hand on Marcus's shoulder,

"Arthur will you please leave, I have nothing to admit," Marcus said with frustration.

"Marcus you really changed!" Arthur exclaimed this because he is bullying Marcus and Marcus did not burst out in anger, He looks sadder, not angry.

"Stop this rubbish and leave," Marcus shouted.

"Ok, I will talk sensible," Arthur smiled,

"I had checked all her reports and my doctor, who is treating Olivia told me that she is recovering well, and medicines are working super-fast. She will be back on her foot soon, no need to worry." Arthur explained.

Marcus heaves a sigh of relief hearing that a small smile crept over his lips.

"I heard, what you said doctor, Now leave," Marcus said while opening the door and raised his hand to signal him to get out.

Arthur walked out the room waving his hand,

Marcus closed the door picked out his cell phone and called Tom,

"Tom, did you find any information?" He ruthlessly asked.

"Master, there is no missing report that has been registered for Olivia so far. Moreover, the team didn't find any news about Cox," Tom obediently answered.

"How can that be possible? Does nobody bother about missing Olivia? although she is a princess." Marcus frowned.

"I regret to say that master she is not a princess, and she lived her life in an orphanage." Tom calmly conveyed the message,

Marcus' face turns red because of anger, and he shouted, "How it could be possible? We have confirmed that Cox has a daughter named Olivia,"

"You are right master," Tom professionally said,

"Master, we are trying too hard to find King cox and we will soon present him in front of you".

"I need action," Marcus yelled at him and disconnected.

He slammed his phone on the wall in anger and the phone smashed into pieces.

He opened his laptop and ran his fingers rapidly on the keyboard, he was checking his company website.

 He was too fed up with all the kidnapping and revenge now he wants to focus on his business,

He is a workaholic and loves to work although this revenge is something very important than work. This girl is getting on to his nerves also he just wanted to finish and get rid of this girl as soon as possible.

He closed his eyes and leaned his back on the sofa, trying to calm himself,

As he calmed down, he got a glimpse of Olivia crying in pain, He immediately opened his eyes,

"What's that?" he asked himself,

"How can I sense her?"

He again closed her eyes and sensed her again, his heart twitched,

"Arthur is my twin brother and I tried so hard to sense him so many times with the wizardly powers, but I never succeeded, then how can I sense her being with her only for four days?"

He hurriedly stood up from the chair and walked to the bathroom had a quick shower, dressed up professionally and rushed to his company in his Lamborghini.

He drove down the valley leaving behind the woods, he pushed the breaks outside a tall building having an "M&M group of company" looking at the brand hoarding his face glowed up with proud,

His blue eyes sparkled, he entered the building, everyone stood and bowed him,

He did not address anyone and arrogantly walked to his private elevator Tom who was waiting for him outside the elevator. Tom submissively followed him to the elevator, and both entered the elevator, his office is on the 25th floor,

"Master, there is bad news." Tom stood by him lowering his head,

Marcus creased his forehead raising his brows at him.

"Do you really expect me to listen to you? you useless fellow," he yelled.

"I am afraid to say this Master, but I request you please be patient and it could help you," Tom words trembled, he clenched his fist tightly,

Marcus raised his hand, and Tom proceeded.

"Master, King Cox's Kingdom was attacked by Kingdom Dragon 15 years back, that time Olivia was only 5 years old. Rumors are that the entire royal had been killed by the dragons or escaped the attacked successfully."

"Through our reliable sources, I get to know that, since then nobody saw any of the Cox family members,"

CHAPTER-7 "A LITTLE GUEST"

The elevator stopped on the 25th floor, Marcus angrily walked, and Tom quietly followed him,

This floor is a private floor of Marcus. A huge office is painted white, and a big portrait of the King is hanging on the front wall, he is Marcus's father. He walked straight to the portrait raised his head looking at his father's portrait with respect, he closed his eyes to offer him prayers.

He turned back to his table, it's a wide wooden table with a big leather chair on its side., he sat on his chair and started rolling his hands on the paper holder, Tom was standing behind him submissively lowering his head and clenching his hand in a fist.

Marcus was intensely thinking, "Do you really think Cox is dead, Tom?" He suspiciously asked, his anger has somehow calmed so far,

"Master, we are looking for the pieces of evidence to prove his death and one more information, I just received is that the diamond crystal is deactivated till date and still drowned in the magical pond,"

"If Cox's kingdom had been demolished, then the magic crystal would have destroyed itself. Its presence indicates that Cox still has their existence, maybe an heir or heiress who successfully escaped the attack," Tom clearly explained every aspect.

"Hmm..." Marcus was still thinking about all the aspects, suddenly words of Arthur echoed in his head "She is Innocent".

He raised an eyebrow, "How would Arthur know that she is not the real princess?" he murmured.

"Checkout Arthur last month activities, I want all the information, where and how he spent his single second on my desk by tomorrow?" he harshly ordered.

"Yes, Master," Tom nodded,

Tom was about to walk out of the office,

"Get me a new phone," Marcus ordered him before he left,

Tom took a few steps back and opened a drawer of the side table, the drawer is full of the latest I-phones, he picks one and switched it on and handed it to Marcus,

He is an angry bird and has a habit of smashing his things, his mobile is mainly the victim of his anger whether it's a personal or professional problem, his phone got smashed,

Tom made this drawer, especially for his phones. All phones in the drawer have the clonal sim card of Marcus contact number. This drawer is upgraded with the latest mobile phones every month.

"May I go, Master"? Tom gently asked.

Marcus signalled him to leave with his hand, and Tom stepped out of the room,

Marcus looked down at his phone, he was impatiently scrolling his fingers on the phone screen, searching for something,

After a couple of moments, there is a knock at the door, "Come in", he ordered without raising his head,

A man entered with a file in his hand. He is Fin, Marcus's official personal assistant and looks after his business affairs in his absence,"

"Good morning, Master," Fin bowed to Marcus,

Marcus who was still scrolling his phone screen didn't look up at him,

"Master, Mr. Tyrant Wright is waiting for you at the meeting hall with his new plan for the merger."

Marcus raised his head, stood up, and started moving to the door, 'Let's go Fin." He ordered while moving, Fin rushed to the door and opened it for him, Marcus stepped out and Fin followed him,

"Master, I have gone through his proposal, Mr. Tyrant has explained everything clearly. The land on which he wants to construct an Ambience Mall belongs to Smith's empire and cost trillions of pounds If we leased the land to Wright's groups of companies, we could earn huge revenue from the barren land. The land is out of use after the demise of King-Smith", Fin explained

Marcus subconsciously nodded his head still looking on his phone screen, his facial expressions keep on changing while looking on the phone screen. More to Fin's surprise his arrogant and rude Master slightly smiled twice in the span of 5 minutes, Fin was amazed to see him smile.

Fin is serving the Kingdom Smith since his birth. His ancestors served the king and the responsibility of serving the Kingdom was hereditarily moved to Fin.

He never saw Marcus smile like this, "What is he watching on the phone"? Fin anxiously thought...

In Smith's Mansion,

Olivia woke with a small pat on her face, she opened her eyes to see who is patting, there is a cute little girl sitting on her side, her big black eyes are amusingly staring at Olivia.

"Who are you?" Olivia asked rubbing her eyes,

The maid who was cleaning the room looked at Olivia and helped her to sit,

The little girl kept looking at Olivia,

"Hi, I am Alice," she innocently said raising her hand towards Olivia,

"I am Olivia nice to meet you, Alice", both shake hands with a bright smile,

"She is Charity, my mom," Alice introduced the maid to Olivia,

"Oh, your mom, you are so cute Alice, Olivia pinched Alice's cute little nose," Alice smiled looking at her,

"Alice, don't disturb the lady," Charity scolded her.

"Miss, Shall I help you get clean"? Charity politely asked.

Olivia looked at her and then sadly rolled her eyes on her fractured arm and bandaged feet, "But, I can't walk to the washroom" she said.

"Don't worry Miss, I will help you," She bought a wheelchair for her and helped Olivia sit on the wheelchair and pushed the wheelchair to the washroom,

"Alice, don't touch anything and behave okay," Charity instructed Alice while pushing the wheelchair in the washroom.

Alice cutely nodded and waved her hand; both exchanged a warm smile.

Olivia felt good to have Alice as a little guest in this room,

Charity helped her shampoo her long red hair, gave her a sponge bath as she had bandages on her feet, put on a beautiful pink cotton midi, which is very comfortable for Olivia,

Both came out of the washroom.

Charity rolled the wheelchair in front of a dressing mirror. Olivia looked at the mirror her wounds and scratches on her arms have slightly faded, she was saddened looking at her pale face and weak body,

The maid took off the towel from her wet head, miss "Shall I use a hairdryer to dry up your hair?"

Olivia kept looking at herself in the mirror and swept in her past.

Olivia lived the life of an orphan and never had a servant to serve her.

In an orphanage every child works on their own, when she was fifteen years old she started working part-time, she worked at many places for a few pounds and hardly earn her monthly expenses. She got her graduation degree on her 20th Birthday and was too excited. As a graduate, she has many opportunities to work with MNC's and can earn a good salary but when she went to that shop to buy sweets for her fellow orphans she was kidnapped, her dreams and desires went in vain. A tear dribbled down her eyes thinking of all that has happened to her so far,

Alice jumped out of the bed and stood by her wheelchair,

Her little soft hands wiped Olivia's tears and "Is this hurting you?"

Alice sweetly asked pointing to Olivia' plastered hand.

Olivia came back from her thoughts and looked at Alice faking a smile,

"No, my doll, it is not at all hurting," Olivia pretends to be calm in front of Alice, but deep inside her heart, her soul is much more hurt than her body.

Charity switched on the hairdryer and rolled the hairdryer all over her head till the hair are completely dried. She tied her long red hair in a high ponytail and put a cute hair tie on it,

Alice who was amazingly looking at Olivia raised her toes and pinched Olivia's nose, "You are so cute Olivia!"

She exclaimed pouting her lips, same as Olivia did to her before,

Both burst out in a laugh.

Olivia leans on her and kissed Alice's cheeks,

This was the scene that Marcus was watching on his mobile phone all the time when Fin was explaining to him the meeting agenda,

Olivia's room has a hidden camera installed and Marcus has its exclusive access, though he can sense Olivia, he preferred CCTV footage as it is live and clear,

He is subconsciously getting drawn to Olivia and felt something for her. Her tears made him sad and looking at her pink smiling lips he smiled, which Fin noticed.

CHAPTER-8 "THE GOLDEN BOX"

Fin opened the conference hall door for Marcus.

"Master, Mr. Wright is here," Fin informed.

Marcus put the phone down on the table and took his seat,

"Be seated Mr. Wright," Marcus ruthlessly said without even looking at Tyrant who stood in respect to bow him,

Meeting started...

In Smith's Mansion,

Olivia peacefully had her breakfast, Charity fed her spoon by spoon and Alice kept smiling looking at her,

"Would you like to have something to eat Alice?" Olivia asked.

"No, I already had my breakfast," she evitablely answered.

"Oh really?" Olivia confirmed looking at her innocent eyes,

The nurse came in for a routine check-up and to change Olivia's bandages and the nurse asked Charity and Alice to leave,

Alice hesitated to go out, "Mom I want to stay with Olivia, she needs me," She innocently said,

"No doll, she doesn't need you, let the nurse check her up and we will come back after a while,"

"Olivia, shall I go?" she asked worriedly.

Looking at the innocent face, Olivia permitted her to go as she doesn't want the little girl to get horrified looking at her open wounds.

"Nice to meet you, Alice, see you soon", she waves her hand smiling.

"Ok, Olivia, Nurse please be gentle to her, Alice requests the nurse sweetly,

The nurse nodded and both went out of the room, Olivia's eyes stuck to Alice until the door was closed.

"Miss, please do let me know if it hurts," Nurse politely asked Olivia and started unwrapping her foot bandage.

Olivia was furiously staring at her foot. Her eyes rolled with each layer shoving from her wounds,

When she completely removed the bandages, her feet looked a bit swollen and few blisters were there, they didn't look much hurt, then Marcus words echoed in her head, "stupid doctor wasted so many bandages on her feet,"

She sighed and felt relieved that her feet are fine,

"Miss, your wounds have recovered very well, our medicines suited you well, now there is no need of many bandages, I will just put a single layer, but I regret to say, it will take 2 more days for you to stand on your feet," she professionally consoled and explained her every aspect of treatment.

Olivia was really impressed and wonders that Marcus has his own qualified medical staff and medicine.

"Amazing" she murmured,

The nurse injected her a painkiller and fed two pills in her mouth and asked her to chew,

"Are they chewable?" Olivia asked reluctantly as she hates the bitter taste of medicine,

The nurse smiled and said "don't worry miss. This medicine is different from other human medicines,"

As soon as the pills melt in her mouth, the sweetness of pills tempts her taste buds.

"You guys are really genius! How did you invent such sweet medicines?"

"It's doctor Arthur who invented these medicines, not me."

"Arthur??" she asked with a big question mark on her face,

The nurse ignored her question and helped her to lay down on the bed and covered her with a thin blanket,

"Take care, Miss," she smiled and left the room,

Olivia is feeling good being caressed by so many people around her, Charity, Alice, and this nurse,

She thought of Alice innocent, bubbly, mischievous talks and soon she fell asleep,

Marcus deliberately didn't come to her room for the next two days, as he tried to ignore her,

Marcus made himself stay busy in the company,

Despite being busy, he had his eye on Olivia's recovery,

Tom and his team are collecting information about Arthur last month activities and Olivia's past.

Cameron, who is an undercover agent of Marcus looking for all the important facts about Olivia from the Orphanage.

He got a lot of information that he only wanted to share with Marcus,

He approached Marcus as soon as possible,

He sneaked in Marcus private floor as he can't show up publicly, Tom informed Marcus about Cameron, Marcus who was addressing an important meeting that time, continued his meeting and wrap up the meeting within half an hour and rushed to his office,

Tom followed him, Marcus entered his office, Cameron was standing lowering his head and bowed to Marcus,

Marcus arrogantly leaned on his chair, looked at Cameron,

"Master..., Cameron looked at Tom and hesitates to speak more,"

"You can speak in front of Tom," Marcus understood his hesitation and asked him to proceed,

"Master, I have something for you, and picked out a small golden box from his pocket and presented that to Marcus,"

"What is this"? Marcus curiously asked looking at the box in his hand,

"Answers to all questions are in the box," kindly open it, Cameron sincerely said.

He astonishingly opened the box, his eyes widened, he shockingly stood from his chair and looked at Cameron, "Where did you find this box"? he mumbled.

"Master, the old caretaker of the orphanage where Olivia lived gave me this,"

"Master, He told me that 15 years ago, on a dark stormy night an injured lady knocked at the door of this orphanage.

The man opened the door and was shocked to see an injured woman carrying a 5-year-old unconscious girl in her severely injured arms and pleaded to save the girl,

The man helped them in and first aid the girl, but the woman refused to have the treatment she just wanted him to save the girl, the man allowed them to stay in the orphanage,

The woman left the girl in the orphanage that night and never showed up again,

The man told me that the woman was murmuring Olivia again and again, this is how he got to know that her name is Olivia, this box was lying near Olivia's head when the man found her the next morning,

There was a small note as well, Cameron handed him a piece of paper some blurred words were written on the piece of paper, which is not visible with the naked eyes,

The man kept this box and note secretive till date with a hope that the woman will come again to take her daughter,

The man is never able to read what is written in the note as the script is unknown to him." Cameron said,

Marcus listened to him carefully and smiled viciously looking back at the thing inside the box.

CHAPTER -9 "THE IDENTICAL TWINS"

"What about Arthur?" he impatiently asked raising his eyebrows.

Master Arthur organised a free health check-up in that orphanage last month and he personally stays there for a day, but nothing suspicious about him, he professionally spends his time treating the orphan children.

"Did he encounter Olivia there?" Marcus asked obstructing,

"Master, nobody was sure about that as Master Arthur interacts with everyone might that includes Olivia as well", Cameron said lowering his head in fear,

"Hmm... You did a great job," Cameron.

Marcus appreciated the information and was still thinking of the Arthur ideology behind the medical camp

He gestured to Cameron, to leave and "keep your eyes on that orphanage," he hoarsely ordered him, Cameron obediently nodded and went out of the door and disappeared.

Marcus sighed leaning on his chair and closed his eyes calmly thinking of Olivia,

In Smith Mansion,

In the span of two days, Olivia recovered well, The nurse helped her to stand on her feet and advised her to slowly took a step, although the nurse is supporting Olivia to assure her safety,

Alice who saw Olivia standing on her feet for the first started jumping excitedly, "Yeah, Olivia now you can walk", she shouted joyfully with sparkling eyes,

Olivia smiled brightly looking at Alice, "Yes Alice,"

She walked for 10 minutes around the room her feet are not at all hurting now, just little scars of blisters are there, all the scratches on her body has also healed, now she is looking quite healthier than before but the plaster on her wrist is still intact. The hairline fracture is taking a quite long to heal as expected, Alice has painted few cute faces on that white plaster which made Olivia smile whenever she looks at her plastered wrist.

"Miss, I am glad your feet have healed completely," the nurse said while helping her sit on the bed.

"Thank you dear", It's all because you and Charity caressed me a lot, Olivia thanked both of them and a tear rolled out her eyes, Alice rushed to Olivia and wiped her tears, "You didn't mention my name Olivia, I am angry with you," she frowns cutely,

Olivia leaned to Alice kissed her forehead, "I have no words to thank you, my doll, you did so much for me, now on we are BFFs, okay", Olivia warmly shake hand with Alice, trying to befriend with the little girl,

"Waaoooo, Now I have two BFF in this mansion," Alice smiled and joyfully started jumping,

"Two? Who else is your best friend?" Olivia curiously asked,

"Arthur"..."He will be happy to know", Alice cutely replied and ran out of the room to meet Arthur.

"Olivia is feeling good today. The Nurse collected all the medical equipment which are now useless for Olivia's treatment and put them in a small wooden box, Olivia noticed her and asked, "What's your name?"

"Sorry, earlier I was in so much pain that I forgot to ask you..."

"My name is Eden Dalton", The nurse sincerely answered looking at her,

"Nice name Ms. Dalton,"

"Miss, you can call me Eden" she insists.

Olivia generously glanced at Eden and turned to look at Charity who is cleaning the room,

Everyone is so humble and noble here, "Why can't he be kind to her?

She thought about Marcus, she also realized that it's been 2-3 days since he didn't come to see her? Different thoughts rolling in her head about the place, the kidnapping, she couldn't conclude what this is all about?

"Eden, can you please take this wheelchair out of the room? Its presence made me feel disabled," Olivia gave a hatred look at the wheelchair.

"Certainly, Miss," The Nurse nodded and roll-out the chair out of the room,

The room again looks the same beautiful room, since she got injured, the room looks more like a hospital ward with a slight tinge smell of medicines.

Charity and Eden went out of the room after finishing the cleaning of the room.

Olivia roamed around the room slowly, after a while she stopped near the floor to ceiling window and looked out. The mesmerizing view grabbed her attention.

The verdant forest was so green that it could drip water and it was very eye-catching. But, Olivia narrowed her eyes as if dazzling. A strand of sadness flashed across Olivia's eyes.

Suddenly, Alice entered the room shouting with joy with a cute doll in her hand,

"Hey Olivia, Arthur bought a new doll for me," Olivia jerked coming out from her trance with Alice's chirps.

Alice excitedly grabs Olivia's hand and started pulling her out of the room,

"Alice where are you taking me? Wait, honey," Olivia screamed and pushing herself back,

Before she can stop Alice both step out of the room,

Olivia was pushing herself back but failed to stop Alice, she is quite weak and can't use much force as any jerk can hurt her fractured wrist,

Olivia looked around the corridor, she got scared looking around the corridor and her heart skipped a beat with the flashback visual of last time rolling in front of her eyes,

When she stepped out in this corridor and came back brutally injured and became bedridden for a week,

"Alice, please try and understand I can't roam around like this, please stop." She badgered trying to stop the little girl.

"You can roam anywhere", a cold voice came, both simultaneously turned back and Alice shoved Olivia's hand, Olivia lost her balance and fell in someone arms.

"Arthur," Alice's eyes glittered.

Olivia looked at him. His face is quite like Marcus, but his dark blue eyes are calm and humble, "Someone is having a good time! I guess brother," Marcus walked in the corridor from nowhere and harshly taunted looking at Arthur holding Olivia in his arms,

Arthur and Olivia looked at him embarrassedly. Arthur helped Olivia to stand firmly. Olivia got scared and started fiddling with the hem of the dress lowering her head.

Alice shrugged behind Arthur long legs, Olivia gazed at Alice from the corner of her eyes, "Even kids are afraid of this devil" she thought.

"Brother nothing like that?" Arthur said heading towards Marcus.

As Arthur moved forward, Alice slipped to Olivia frightenedly.

"Brother?" Olivia widened her eyes astonishingly rolling her eyes at Arthur and then turned to Marcus. She was shocked to see an identical twin with different behaviour one is a devil and the other is an angel! She exclaimed in her head,

"Go back to the room," Marcus rudely ordered Olivia, Olivia trembled and grabbed Alice's hand and rushed back to the room,

She is terrified by his words, that she didn't look back at all.

CHAPTER-10 "KILL ME"

Olivia heaved a sigh leaning back to the closed door,

She then looked down at Alice who still looked frightened. Olivia rubbed Alice blonde curls and tries to soothe the little girl,

She took her to the sofa and sat with her,

"Ooh, Alice, your doll is so beautiful," she said pouting trying to divert Alice's attention,

"Is she?" Alice asked looking at the doll...

"Ok, let's give her a name," Olivia demanded taking the doll from Alice's hand,

Alice tapping her small fingers on her chin thinking and glancing at the doll,

"I can't think of any name, I don't know any good girlish name." Alice angrily stomping her foot on the floor.

"Okay, okay, don't worry, Arthur gave you this doll and I will give her a name, so she will become a mutual gift of your BFFs!"...Olivia soothe her anger, kids are so pure that can be moulded anyways she thought looking at Alice glittering eyes with that idea.

"Hmm. How about Luna...?"

"NO, it's a thorny name!"

"Ammy?"

"No."

"Aubree?"

"No"

"Angel?"

"Yes, Alice and her angel"...She clapped while reciting.

"Arthur will be happy to know her name", Alice joyfully screams, running out of the room.

Olive smiles heaving a relaxing sigh.

Arthur entered Marcus room and closed the door,

Marcus stood leaning his back on the wall and his arms folded close to his chest, Arthur standing in front of him with his hands in his pocket,

Both looked into each other eyes,

"Arthur, I never thought my own blood would betray me one day," Marcus agonizingly said breaking the silence.

"What are you saying Marcus? be clear with your words," Arthur demanded pulling out his hands from his pocket and stood firmly, He sensed something fishy...

"Ok, as you say, brother, why did you organize a medical camp in Pinewood orphanage last month?" he gave an ironic gaze to Arthur.

"Marcus, it's none of your business!" Arthur exclaimed calmly looking back into his eyes,

"It wouldn't be my business until it was not related to my revenge," Marcus yelled.

"You did than purposely Arthur?" He scornfully asked.

"No!" Arthur retorted...

"Arthur, don't let me lose my temper just tell me, your purpose behind that, I just want to hear the truth, only the truth." He harshly asked punching the table,

"Marcus, brother listen to me"... Arthur tried to soothe Marcus.

"Try and understand it was a regular medical check-up nothing purposely in that," he is actually afraid of Marcus anger,

"Oh really? then tell me how you knew that girl Olivia is innocent and how come she belongs to the same orphanage?" Marcus enviously asked leaning back on his chair,

Marcus is looking tired as he didn't sleep for 3 days and 3 nights, he was working all the time in the company trying to ignore Olivia.

"Brother, you look so tired, you better rest, nothing to suspicion about the medical camp. It was merely a coincidence," Arthur calmly explained.

"You deliberately did this, so that you can be in mom's good books, right?" he asked.

This time Arthur didn't lie and come up with truth…a half-truth...

"I tried to help you, but I am ashamed of myself, that I couldn't find anything to help," Arthur pushed back the tears that rolled in his eyes looking at tired Marcus yearning for revenge,

Marcus hurriedly walked to Arthur and hugged, "I am so sorry Arthur, I didn't mean to hurt you, why did you hide that from me?"

His anger melted looking at Arthur glistened eyes, he consoled Arthur-like father,

Marcus is five minutes older than Arthur that is why he loved to call himself elder and always loved Arthur-like father though they have their sibling rivalry too,

"It is our revenge brother, and I will never betray you. Mom will be proud of us together. I am never against you. I am against your technics of revenge. Olivia is an orphan till the time I get to know that your men already kidnapped her", Arthur was gently justifying himself,

"Yes, I get to know that she lived the life of an orphan, but she is not an orphan. She is the heiress of the Crystal kingdom! "...Marcus words echoed in the room.

"What?" Arthur was shocked to hear that, "But, king Cox and the royal family were killed by the dragons fifteen years ago," Arthur said in shock,

Marcus raised his eyebrows to Arthur,

"Arthur, I must say, you are not only a medical genius but a brilliant detective too." his compliment is more like a taunt to Arthur.

Arthur understood what he meant but ignored it,

"I knew this from long time but am unable to collect any piece of evidence to prove it so I didn't disclose it to you", Arthur disheartened admitting his failure.

"Forget it," Arthur,

In future, if you have any information, you will first share that with me, we will be mutually on this, Marcus trying to manipulate him.

"Yes, of course", Arthur submissively nodded,

Both the brothers are too smart to fool each other, both are aware of other strengths and weaknesses,

"You better rest brother, see you at dinner," Arthur said and left,

Marcus noticed his body language and understood that Arthur already had information about the golden box as well, if not then why he didn't ask much about the Crystal kingdom and its heiress?

On the other hand, Arthur thought he succeeded in fooling Marcus with his tears,

Marcus walked to Olivia's room,

Olivia heard the footsteps and curled up on the bed, pretending to be asleep,

Marcus opened the door, slowly entered the room, and sat next to her. Olivia didn't move and tried hard not to open her eyes,

Marcus knew she is not sleeping, he still coldly stares at her face her big trembling eyelashes making her look so cute and fragile,

Marcus licked her hair caressed her like never,

He slightly moved his fingers from her hair to her tender cheeks and then to her lips, her face heated up and she immediately stood up,

He deliberately did that to irritate her,

"What do you want?" she screamed.

"Oh, you are not sleeping Sugar candy?" he huffed.

"Marcus, don't call me by that slutty name," she yelled.

His anger infuriated on hearing his name from her. He grabbed her neck and pushed her back to the bed, "How dare you call my name?" he screamed pushing his hand harder on her neck that almost choked her throat with force, her pink face turned white.

He looked at her weeping eyes, as she was getting out of her breath. He loosened his grip and threw her on the bed and walked away from her, hit his palm on the wall writhing in the guilt of unknowingly humiliating her again.

Olivia tries to sit, breathing back and rubbing her numb neck. She coughed gasping heavily looking at Marcus holding her plastered wrist as it jerked when he threw her on the bed,

"Master...," He shockingly looked back at her,

"Can we talk?" she submissively asked...

He couldn't resist her tears and again turned back to the wall, his heart twitched looking at her plastered wrist,

"I don't know why you kidnapped me. I lived a miserable life as an orphan. I don't even know who my parents are? I didn't remember anything as I was just five years old when a woman abandoned me at the orphanage. I couldn't even call her mom as I don't remember how my mother looked. I have no memories of my family." She gasps as tears stream down her cheeks.

She sighed and continued sitting on the edge of the bed,

"You misunderstood me with some other girls, and I am as useless as dead to you," she burst out in sob. "If you still consider, I owe you revenge or this life, then please kill me at once, I can't take it anymore, I want to die," she demanded yelling and sobbing.

She was tired of her life because she struggled so hard to get graduated and when the day arrived, she was dragged into this mess.

She has no aim to live, it's better to die than to be assaulted again and again, nobody bothers whether she is alive or dead.

Her last words and mercy for death stabbed Marcus' heart,

He just wants to end this all as soon as possible.

He fetched an old picture book from the table drawer and slammed in front of her on the bed.

Olivia looked at that picture book,

"Open the book," he ruthlessly ordered her,

She wiped her tears and put her plastered wrist on her laps as it is paining like hell,

She slowly turned the book, looked down at the old pictures, a beautiful palace, she amusedly started turning the pages,

She couldn't recognize any of the pictures. She keeps on turning, trying to remind something. When she reached the last page, her eyes widened looking at the picture of a young couple in royal attire standing in front of the big palace, the lady in the picture was holding an infant. The lady's face looked like Olivia, the man chocolate brown eyes as same as her,

Are they, my parents? She thought and sadly rolled her good hand on the picture and her eyes again fledged.

She is crying in pain looking at the picture and holding her head as she couldn't remember anything,

Marcus, who was continuously looking at her changing expression from amused to sad, snatched the book from her,

She didn't look up and just kept crying,

"Did you recognize anyone in this picture book?" he calmly asked,

She held her chest and tried to control her tears...

"No!"

"Why did you cry looking at last picture?" he questioned again,

"I cried because the couple resembled like me, I imagined them as my parents and crying is an emotional reaction,"

"You cannot understand the pain of a poor orphan because you are a rich person who can play with anyones life anytime," she added.

"You guessed it right they are your actual parents!" he disdainfully left her weeping,

Her eyes widened in shock hearing that revelation, she couldn't ask more as he already walked out of the room, she keeps on sobbing loud.

Marcus pressed the medical emergency button before leaving the room,

A nurse hurriedly entered her room soon after the master left.

CHAPTER-11 "ARTHUR"

Eden rushed to Olivia,

"Miss, what happened?" she asked looking at her crying face.

Olivia didn't reply.

Eden looked down at her sobbing, holding her plastered wrist,

She examined her plaster and found some cracks over it, she hurriedly cut the plaster and was shocked to see her red swollen wrist. She immediately grabs the small x-ray machine and put Olivia's arm on the machine to scan.

Eden was shocked to see the X-ray report,

She picks out her phone to dial Arthur,

"Doctor, the lady broke her wrist," She informed.

Arthur appeared in the fiction of second using his wizardry powers,

He reached Olivia, slides a chair close to her. Eden handed him the   X-ray report, he looked at the X-ray and sighed,

He sat on the chair and took her broken wrist in his hands and started examining it moving up and down. He pressed a point on her red swollen skin and asked, "Is it hurting here, Miss?'

Olivia was sitting frozen, her tears dried up and her red sour eyes giving a traumatic look,

She didn't utter a word,

Arthur understood her situation and wrapped another cast around her wrist, and kept a silicone armrest supported by a belt that hangs around Olivia's neck,

"Are you twins playing a game?" she groaned.

"Sorry, I didn't get you, Miss?" Arthur asked looking at her emotionless face.

"One is humiliating and hurting me and other compensating his sins treating me," she dryly exclaimed.

"I really apologize for Marcus misbehaving. He is so short-tempered and had a bad habit of smashing things in anger," he calmly said wiping his hands with the towel,

"Thing??? Oh, I see, I am a thing to you guys, I am being dumb thinking myself a living being with bone and flesh,"...a tear rolled out from the corner of her eyes, feeling pity for herself,

Arthur was shocked to hear those traumatic words from her,

He cupped her face in his hands, "Olivia look into my eyes," he softly ordered.

Olivia Brown chocolaty eyes bored in his dark blue eyes,

Arthur looks deep into her eyes and is saddened to see the empty sad eyes, "I promise you! Nobody will ever hurt you again, not even Marcus," he strongly assured.

Olivia faked a smile, "Promise?"

Arthur raised his hand towards Charity who just walked in the room with the tray of dinner for Olivia.

The Charity handed him a bowl of hot chicken soup,

Arthur took a spoon full of soup and blew it slowly to check before raising it to Olivia's mouth, Olivia shoves it and soup drops splash on the floor,

He again took the spoon, blew it and raised to her, she stubbornly shoving it, again and again, now the drops of soup turned into a pool of soup on the floor,

Arthur patiently trying to feed her, without saying anything,

The bowl was empty now, he looked back at the tray and took a bowl of veg noodles, the tempting smell of spices and herbs watered Olivia's mouth, but she still behaved like a stubborn spoiled girl, refusing to eat.

"Miss, please eat, else you will starve," Arthur requested her,

"It is better to die starving than getting humiliated!" she exclaimed.

Olivia is actually starving, and the delicious smell of food paced her cravings,

"Ms. Olivia, I request you please be gentle to me, eat something," He squeezes his eyes like a small boy,

"Okay, tell me what you like to eat the most?" he put the tray of food on his laps in front of Olivia, his knees rubbed on Olivia's legs and spark ran down his spine, he never felt this ever before, he raised his head and curiously looked at Olivia innocent face, poor girl, he thought.

Olivia looked down at the food, porridge, noodles, grilled chicken, and a chocolate cupcake, she subconsciously licked her lips,

Arthur noticed her gaze and took a spoon poke that in the cupcake and raise towards her mouth,

This time Olivia couldn't resist and opened her mouth to eat.

Arthur fed her everything, to his surprise she was famished, she ate all the cupcakes and noodles. She wanted to eat the grilled chicken as well, but she burped loudly and felt embarrassed and refused to eat more,

She looked around at Eden, Charity and Arthur, they all burst out in a laugh.

Olivia laughing her heart out. Arthur's eyes sparkled to see Olivia's enchanting smile and her chocolaty brown eyes glows like a gem,

He helped Olivia to lay on the bed, covered her legs with the thin blanket and sat on the chair close to her head holding and rubbing her non-plastered hand,

"I am sorry Master Arthur," Olivia muttered looking at the ceiling,

"Hey, little girl, don't call me master, I hate that word," he pinched her nose, "I am sorry to you,"

Arthur has treated thousands of girls but never felt so warm for anyone like he started feeling for Olivia meeting her for the first time,

"I am not a little girl anymore, I am grownup, I am 20 years old economics graduate but he ruined everything," her anguish tone made him feel sad for what Marcus did to her,

"I visited pinewood orphanage last month, I met everyone there but didn't see you how?" he asked deliberately changing the topic.

"Why did you go there, to kidnap me before your brother?" she questioned.

"No, not at all, my hospital organized a medical camp for the orphans," he calmly answered,

"I worked in a double shift in a restaurant morning, evening and in between I was studying in the university, so to save time and to earn more money without missing my classes, many times I slept outside the restaurant or stayed with my friend Jade. I visit the orphanage rarely these days. Who cares about an orphan? her words pierced him,

Shit, I again made her sad, he thought, started a new conversation,

Alice told me you gave her doll, a name, "Angel" both simultaneously said,

She smiled thinking of Alice. "She is a darling girl."

"Her naughty cute eyes brighten up my life for a while,"

Both talked about Alice a lot and Olivia started blinking her sleepy eyelids. Arthur leaned on her side on the bed, patting her forehead as he does to Alice when she couldn't sleep on her own,

Olivia murmured sleepily... "I love you Aaa," and fell asleep,

Arthur looked at her sleepy innocent face and subconsciously kissed her forehead and slept next to her to take care of her.

CHAPTER-12 "A GIFT"

Olivia woke up early because of the uncomfortable strap around her neck she couldn't sleep for long. She was stunned to see Arthur sleeping next to her,

"Why did he sleep here?" she thought. It's his mansion where ever he can sleep... "hmm,"

She slowly slides down the bed and walked into the washroom,

She was not feeling sleepy at all and roamed in the room as she doesn't want to disturb Arthur in his sleep.

Sunshine was dazzling down the curtains,

She moved towards the window and stood behind the curtains without removing them aside, looking down the dense lush green valley, the pine trees look more beautiful from here, it's like God has given the best of natural beauty to this place,

Arthur woke up and he rolled his hand on the bed where Olivia was sleeping, rubbing his eyes with the other hand,

He dreadfully stood from the bed as he didn't find Olivia sleeping there,

He looked around but didn't find her anywhere in the room. He then suddenly saw a shadow behind the curtains. A smile crept over his lips.

"Is someone hiding from me?" he removed the curtains and Olivia trembled with his sudden words,

"Ooo, you" ...she jerked with his sudden words

"Why you woke up so early? was I snoring so loud that it disturbed you?" he jittered.

She grins, "Not at all Arthur, I even didn't realize that you are sleeping next to me,"

"I couldn't sleep because of this strap, it is quite uncomfortable," she said adjusting the strap of the cast,

Arthur moved close to her to examine and found red rashes around her neck,

"Ohh, girl, you are so sensitive," Arthur said looking at the few rashes that have developed on your skin,

He carefully removed the strap from her neck and touched on the rash over her skin to examine the neck, a spark went down his spine with his fingers touching her naked skin, he was so close to Olivia, that her cold breathes fan his arms, he immediately removed his hand and took a step back.

"Don't worry, I will send Eden with an ointment and another soft strap," he said turning to the door and hurriedly treads out the room ranking his black curls,

Olivia walked to the mirror and started looking at the rashes in the mirrors, her eyes landed on the red prints on her neck reminding of Marcus forcefully strangled her neck when she called his name, "They are not rashes," she murmured,

"Devil"

Charity stepped into the room,

"Good morning, Miss," She bowed to Olivia who is still standing in front of the mirror talking to herself,

Olivia smiles to see her, "How are you, Charity?" She humbly asked.

"I am good, Miss, thank you for asking,"

"How's your wrist now?" Charity asked looking at her new cast,

"It will be fine soon, I hope!" she exclaimed holding her wrist.

Charity helps her with bathing and made her put on the new clothes.

The huge pink closet is full of all the expensive branded dresses, gowns, midis, denim, shorts, night wears so on.

Olivia looked at the closet and then turned her eyes to the overloaded shoe rack with stylish shoes, ballerinas, flats, wedges and what not.

She was amused to see so much branded stuff around the room that too only for her,

"Who designed this room?" she asked sipping her hot chocolate milk,

"Master Marcus," Charity sincerely answered,

"For whom?" she sounds excited this time,

"For you, Miss," Charity smiled.

"Please don't lie, Charity, I know nobody can be so concerned to me, especially not Marcus, oops Master Marcus," she said frightenedly looking at the door,

She doesn't want her other hand to get plastered,

"Where is Alice?" Olivia asked joyfully.

"She has gone out with Master Arthur for shopping," Charity replied cleaning the room.

"Wow, shopping!"

She looked back at the pink closet,

There was a time when I was free to go wherever I wish, but at that time I never had anything good to wear so I always avoid hanging out with others, Now I have branded clothes and shoes, but I am prisoned here,

"How poor I am?" sadness clouded her eyes.

She again strolls towards the window. This floor to ceiling window is her favourite spot in this room, as she can see the dense green forest, she can feel the breeze and the small stream falling down the valley made it worth watching all day.

She trails down memory lane. Where once in her school days, they got a chance to trek a small mountain, she couldn't join the class because she couldn't afford sports shoes and her teacher refused to take her in regular old shoes,

Charity cleaned the room and looked at Olivia standing near the window,

"Miss, I have cleaned the room. Is there anything, I can help you with?" she politely asked,

"Can you take me out to the small stream?" Olivia said pointing out of the window.

"I really apologize miss, I can't do that,"

"I know, that is ok, soon I will be habitual to live in this room."

"You can go, Charity," she said faking a smile.

Charity bowed to her and walked out with the soiled stuff,

Olivia looked around the room again, but nothing to do, she thought of that picture book that Marcus gave her,

A bulb of light glowed over her head,

"Where did he kept that book?" she excitedly opens the pink closet and turned around all the clothes, one by one checked all the drawers,

But, she didn't find that picture book. "I want to see that picture book," she frowned and frustratedly slammed the closet door and the clothes she just stuffed in came out the closet and scattered on the floor,

"Oh shit," she looked down and panicked to see the mess.

She hurriedly grabbed all the clothes and stuffed them back, and closed the closet door,

Suddenly Alice entered in screaming Olivia's name,

Olivia frighteningly turned supporting the closet door with her back pushing the door,

Arthur came in following Alice with so many shopping bags in his hands,

"Olivia, see what I got for you?" Alice joyfully screamed at Olivia's hand but Olivia hesitated to move as she knows, if she moves from here all the clothes will scatter again on the floor,

Arthur noticed Olivia's hesitation and thought, she is afraid of him,

"Alice come here," He called putting down the bags on the sofa,

Alice joyfully picks one bag and dig her small hand in the bag to fetch out a purple Barbie dress, "Arthur gifted me this,"

Olivia faking a smile, "Nice darling,"...Arthur took six bags and walked towards Olivia, "Olivia this is for you," Arthur smiled waving the bags in front of her.

"For me?" she surprisingly yelled.

CHAPTER -13 "A NEW MARCUS"

After a couple of moments. The washroom door opened, Alice and Arthur turned their eyes at Olivia who was standing in front of the washroom door,

Both were stunned to see her. The dress perfectly fitted her, perfectly exposing her curves. She has a god gifted beauty that never needs any makeup to flaunt.

Her naturally pink lips, slightly rosy cheeks and the perfect blunt nose with big chocolaty eyes that she winks at her occasionally, long red hair sliding down her waist "God has carved her patiently."

Arthur stood from the sofa impulsively treading towards Olivia,

He amusingly rolled his eyes around her body from head to toe,

"Alice..., "Do you know this beautiful girl?" he stunningly asked Alice,

Alice also joined Arthur and pouted, "Olivia, YOU LOOK STUNNING," Alice's joyfully yelled and her big black eyes glowered...

"Really?" Olivia amusedly asked looking at both,

"Thank you, Arthur,"... she sincerely thanked him.

She never got a chance to flaunt her beauty like this, she never thought that she could look beautiful.

"Arthur..., let's take Olivia out to the garden!" Alice cutely demanded.

"No!" Olivia is frightened to go out,

Arthur sensed her fear,

"If you want to go out, you can go, you are free to roam around, nobody will stop you," He promisingly said holding Olivia's hand looking deep into her dark brown eyes,

Olivia heartbeat paced up with his words and his blue eyes keep boring into her browns,

Suddenly, Olivia slightly pushed him back and shoved his hand. Before Arthur could understand what happened, Marcus opened the door and entered the room.

"You guys are having real fun!" He frowned looking around the room, the clothes he bought were scattered around the room and some shopping bags lying on the sofa, which made him feel shocked and hurt at the same time,

And, when his eyes landed on Olivia, his eyes glowered and stunningly stared her for a minute and walked to her tip-toed minding the scattered stuff on the floor,

"This is none of those dresses which I bought for you sugar candy!" He exclaimed.

Olivia shrugged and angrily clenched her hands into a fist, digging her nails into her palms.

"I bought this for her,"...Arthur interrupted...

"You should better buy her a new closet as well," Marcus angrily said rolling his eyes on the shopping bags.

Marcus assumed Olivia deliberately throws out the dresses he bought and made space in the closet for what Arthur bought for her today.

"What?" Marcus, don't start that in front of Alice," Arthur growls back at him.

Marcus turned his eyes towards Alice and Alice scarcely ran out of the room.

"You can flirt with my woman in front of that little girl, and I can't express my pain for that?" Marcus continued

"Pain??" "Did you know how much pain she has gone through so far because of you?" Arthur yelled at Marcus pointing at Olivia's cast, anger infuriating in his eyes

Marcus didn't notice that because he was lost in her beautiful face, he turned to Olivia, Olivia trembled and took a step back as Marcus took a step towards her,

He touched her cast, the anger that was pumping through his veins a moment ago is replaced by emotion,

Olivia shrugs clenching her dress with her other hand.

Her eyes lashes trembling because of fear, she is almost shivering with his touch,

 "You freak, you are again hurting her," Arthur frowned and immediately shoved his head, Olivia frightenedly moved behind Arthur,

"Can you please leave Arthur, I want to talk to her privately," Marcus demanded gazing at her,

"No, I won't leave her!" He retorts covering her behind him.

"Oh, have you started feeling for her?" he shamelessly asked smirkingly looking at Olivia who is tightly holding Arthur's hand,

Arthur followed his gaze and looked down, shocked to see Olivia holding his hand and trembling in fear. He covered her hand with his other hand, "I promised her that nobody will hurt her again" and he actually fulfilling his promise to protect her.

"I can also promise you that, will you leave then?" he sounds honest.

Arthur knew that "Marcus is a man of his word and if he promised he will never break that,"

He patted Olivia's hand, softly unwrapped her hand from his and raised her chin, "I am standing outside, he will not hurt you I can assure that,"

Olivia pitifully looked into his eyes as if she is saying "don't go".

Arthur walked out of the room,

Olivia started trembling and slowly taking steps back to move away from Marcus.

Marcus does notice that he squatted down and grab all the scattered clothes from the floor and put them on the bed, he started picking each dress, detangled them and mannerly arranged them in the closet, "Now it looks better!" he exclaimed rolling his sight inside the closet and look back at Olivia,

"I must say, Arthur also has good taste in woman clothing. None of these matches to what you are wearing, so you can keep it as well, but you dare not throw out what I have bought for you," he softly warned her, and a smile crept over his lips.

He was behaving so cool and calm, that she couldn't believe her eyes, she scratched her forehead in confusion and Marcus closed the closet and walked to the sofa,

"Oh... what else did he bought for you? Let me check." he chuckled.

He grabbed the bags and turned them upside down and the stuff scattered on the sofa, he picked every dress, shoes and shoved them one by one. "Nice, nice, nice, everything Arthur bought will suit you, you can keep it but not in this closet, I will send Charity in to arrange them for you."

Olivia shockingly keeps on looking at him,

"The clothes fell out of the closet by mistake and because of my injured wrist I couldn't rearrange them back, I didn't mean that." she honestly justifies herself.

"It's ok, I don't need any justification," he said, but inside his heart, he feels satisfied hearing that.

"Master, can I go to the garden?" she submissively asked.

Her honey-coated words echoed in his ears, he spins and walked towards her, wrapped his hands around her waist pulled her closed to him and rolled his fingers on her pink cheeks moving to her neck, his warm mint breath falls on her lips, he clips his lips to her and slightly kissed her, soon the kiss deepens, she tried hard to push him back but she failed, a tear rolled out of pain as he pressed her plastered wrist,

He senses her pain, and takes a step back loosening his grip around her waist,

"Did I hurt you?" he worriedly asked looking down at her wrist.

"No"...she answered.

"Then, why did you cry?" he sounds strange this time worried and concerned.

She touched her red swollen lips lowering her head,

He immediately cupped her face..." look into my eyes, Oliv".

Butterflies started floating in her stomach hearing her name for the first time, his devilish eyes are pouring love on her, the lust for revenge has faded, she was surprisingly looking into his eyes,

"I will keep my promise, I will never hurt you again" and you are free to roam around the mansion, my sugar candy." He kissed her forehead and walked out of the room,

Olivia couldn't believe her ears and in the span of ten days, it is the first time that he went out of the room without hurting or harassing her.

Chapter-14 "PRIVATE LAKE"

Olivia immediately put on a pair of flats and excitedly ran towards the door,

Arthur was standing sincerely outside the door as he promised,

Arthur was stunned to see Olivia,

"Are you okay?" he nervously asked.

"I am fine!"...she exclaimed smiling.

"Where is Alice?" she asked looking around.

"Might be in the garden", he thoughtfully replied,

"Arthur, can you take me there?"

"Sure!"

Both walked down to the garden,

Olivia amusedly looking around the mansion. She was amazed to see the carved ceilings, velvet curtains, expensive carpets covering the marble floor, the number of servants roaming and working in the mansion.

Arthur took her to a lush green well-maintained garden,

This garden is quite different from the usual garden people have in the city. This garden has all the natural pine trees perfectly trimmed.

Suddenly Olivia saw Alice running behind the beautiful, colourful butterflies.

"Alice"..., Olivia excitedly called her,

Arthur's eyes sparkled with joy looking at Olivia smiling face.

"Hey Olivia, I am so glad to see you," Alice ran to them yelling joyfully, yelling.

She grabbed Olivia's hand and starts pulling her to a place,

"Come Olivia, I will take you at my favourite place."

"Hey, Alice, please be gentle to her, she is injured," Arthur politely said to Alice,

"Sorry, Arthur," she replied.

They saunter through a natural avenue of trees, it is shady, dark, and cool with almost cold. As they come to the end of the trees it opens up into a lake. The air is warmer, the sounds of insects are almost too loud. The lake seems like a black void, the sun bouncing off its surface.

A plopping sound as a fish breaks the surface and ripples widening out. They are at the edge of the lake now, the pebbles underfoot, crunch, a moorhen is disturbed and runs off along the banking, distracting her from its nest. A Kestrel attracted by the disturbance hovers above the next field. The smell, of water and 'ozone', warmth and living.

Alice took her to the shore of a beautiful lake; Olivia was stunned to see a private lake.

"You own a lake?" she amusedly asked Arthur,

"We own this kingdom dear!" he whispered smirkingly.

"Oh, certainly, you are a prince. Perks of being rich," She muttered astonishingly looking around and saw two boats at the shore,

This is a natural lake with so many beautiful white and pink lotuses floating on the water,

She sat down on the edge of the water on a small rock and peer into its depths, she only sees pondweed and small insects at first. As she remains still, layers of water somehow become apparent, the open light layer with minnows darting about, the next darker layer, a large carp is sitting, watching her as she watches him. Then the dark bottom of the pond, the brown silt moving with life.

The dragonflies catch her attention, landing on a bull-rush nearby. She lifts her gaze for a moment to see them in their metallic blue finery. From the corner of her eye, she sees a shape move in the water. She looks back and realises there are loads of fish, her eyes sparkled as she never seen so many fishes before, she saw their black shapes but did not recognise them as fish. There is another pop sound and concentric circles form on the lake, a Moorhen runs away startled.

Though the water was still, with the breezes small waves pop up,

Her eyes glittered to see a wonderful view, Alice was running behind the butterflies and Arthur looking at Olivia's happy gestures, his heart overwhelmed with satisfaction,

Suddenly a tear rolled down her cheeks,

Arthur leaned and hurriedly put his palm down her cheeks and caught the tear, he saw a crystal-clear drop of tears on his palm, his satisfied heart trembled with another drop of tear,

He closed his palms holding her tears,

"Why are these tears, Olivia?" he asked sitting next to her,

"You both are so blessed, you have everything that meant to live a good life,"

"On the other hand, I don't even know who I am? Who are my parents? I have no clues about my existence," and saying that she loudly burst out in tears, keeps on sobbing palming her face.

"Your brother showed me a picture book and he claimed that the royal couple in a picture is my parents, I even couldn't recognize them,"

"I don't even remember that woman who abandoned me, how she looks? Who was she?"

"My existence has no evidence and how can I be happy?" tears kept streaming down her eyes.

Arthur crouched in front of her on the rocks, tightly held her hands and tried to calm her down,

He was shocked to hear that Marcus has shown her a picture book, but right now, he gave priority to calm her down,

"Olivia, please don't cry, I will, and we both will definitely help you find your family. We will never let you down, your existence is important for me, for Alice, for everyone around you." Arthur said.

"No! No..."

She screamed crying. Arthur tightly hugged her and tried to soothe her,

She somehow felt a warmth in Arthur's arms, slowly calms down,

He softly palmed his face and wiped her tears, "You dare not cry again, I can't handle your tears", his eyes glistened saying that,

He softly kissed her forehead and leaned his forehead on hers,

Both silently sit closed feeling each other warmth,

"Olivia...."

Suddenly they heard Alice screaming,

Olivia and Arthur immediately stood from the rock and Arthur helped Olivia to carefully tread through the rocks,

"Olivia, see I caught a beautiful butterfly," Alice joyfully screams.

Arthur and Olivia heaved a sigh of relief and smiled.

"Oh, Alice, you scarred us!" Arthur sneered taking Alice in his arms and kissed her on the cheek, "Don't scream like this again, you sound scary," he chuckled.

Their giggles echoed in the garden.

CHAPTER-15 "SUCCEEDING"

"Did she again cry, Arthur?" Alice furiously asked looking at Olivia's sore eyes

"Yes, Alice", Arthur pouted.

"Olivia, aren't you happy to see the lake?" her eyes filled with sadness,

"I am happy darling!" Olivia patted Alice's cheeks with affection,

"Then why did you cry?" She scowls.

Arthur raised his eyebrows at Olivia in a teasing manner,

Olivia looked at him mischievously smirking,

"I promise you, Alice, I will try not to cry again", Olivia promised.

"You better not cry"...Alice demanded, and they all strolled back to the mansion,

Olivia is feeling a bit tired as she walked for so long after many days of rest and because of her cast, she felt stiffness in her casted arm,

The garden is huge, and the mansion has so many stairs to climb on.

Arthur saw her discomforted facial expressions and asked concerning,

"Are you tired, Olivia?"

Hearing Arthur concerned words, emotions welled up in her eyes, that he can read his gestures as well, how much concern he is for her, she thought.

"Actually, I won't lie, I am totally drained and I..." she paused.

Arthur put Alice down and told her to go back to her cottage,

Alice nodded obediently and waved to Olivia running down the stairs,

"If you want, you can rest on the sofa, we will go back to your room later," Arthur said pointing her towards the drawing hall,

Olivia couldn't resist and agreed to rest,

"Excuse me, Olivia, you better rest here, I will be back soon,"

Arthur excused her and walked somewhere in the mansion, Olivia's eyes gazed at him until he went behind the door,

Olivia leaned her back on the sofa, tiredly closing her eyes to relax after a while Arthur came back with a tray of food and beverages.

"Miss," Olivia opened her eyes and straightens up,

"This is for you Miss Olivia," Arthur is behaving like a butler serving her,

She smirked looking at him,

"Fresh fruit juice for the beautiful, tired girl," Arthur chuckled offering her a glass of fresh juice,

"Thank you," She took the glass and sip the juice,

"Nice" she sneered raising the glass up,

"Would you like to have some snacks, miss?" he politely asked.

Olivia looked at the tray of food and picks a small bowl of nachos, as she is the biggest fan of nachos,

She eats one and closes her eyes feeling the taste of spices,

"Yummy!" She smoldered tempting her taste buds.

She sipped the juice again and kept on enjoying the snacks, then she raised her eyes to Arthur who is still standing by her with his hands clenched in fist like an obedient butler,

"Arthur, Will you please join me?"

Arthur nodded taking a seat next to her on a sofa, she handed her another glass of juice from the tray, and both started chit-chatting enjoying the snacks,

"How big is this mansion?" she curiously asked

"This mansion has 10 floors, the 5 floors are like a basement under the valley, where I run my hospital, five floors over the valley are where we live, he sincerely explained.

"We????"

"Me, Marcus and our mo...Er... our maids," he flustered.

He seems hiding something from her.

"Now you also," he said smiling.

Olivia kept asking him more and more until she tiredly fell asleep on the sofa,

He took her in his arms horizontally and walked to her room. She is in deep sleep and Arthur didn't want her to be disturbed, he softly put her on the bed covered her with a quilt and carefully "Sleep well" he said licking her hair,

He wanted to stay longer with her, but he must go, his profession is calling him. It's almost afternoon and he hasn't gone to his hospital,

Arthur stared at her for a while and reluctantly went out of the room,

Olivia saw him going out and immediately got out of the bed. She wasn't asleep she was just pretending. Now, as she knew each and every small detail about this mansion...

"It's Showtime!"...she accentuated rubbing her hands,

She opened the door and peeked out of her head to check. Only servants are roaming here and there,

As now she is free to roam around, she thought of sneaking out on the private floor of Arthur and Marcus. She calmly walked to the elevator and went to the private floor,

Ding!

The elevator stopped and the door slides open, she walked out of the elevator and looked around,

To her surprise this floor is different from hers, she stepped into a long and wide corridor,

She slowly and slowly strolling in the corridor and saw a line of doors. She attentively walked to the first door opened and peeked in that, then immediately went to the other door, opened it and checked, she was searching for someone, as she opened the last door,

"What are you doing here?" She jerked with a familiar voice coming close to her,

She snaps and immediately turned to him, "O Master…." she flutters.

Marcus came close to her.

"Are you looking for someone Olivia?" Marcus asked for closing the door she just opened,

"Hmm," A knot went down her throat,

"I am looking for Alice...hmm yes,..."

"Servants don't live here, they have separate cottages in the backyard," He smoothly answered,

"Oh, I am sorry Master, I didn't know that"...she stammers.

"Are you still afraid of me?" he asked stepping close to her,

She took a step back lowering her head,

Marcus didn't force her to answer,

"Let me direct you back to your room," he said signalling her to move,

She reluctantly moves with him, and a small smile crept over her lips looking back at the door,

Though she saw an old woman sleeping on a queen size bed in this room her curiosity grew more though her motive is half accomplished, she is quite satisfied,

Both stepped into the elevator.

Chapter-16 "WE WILL WIN"

"I heard you had a good time with Arthur in the morning." he started a conversation breaking the silence.

Marcus was already drawn towards her, he stalks at her often, but he must resist his feelings,

"Yes, he took me to the garden and then Alice took me to the lake", her words were calm and she submissively answering him,

They took the elevator, and apparently, they are both alone in the elevators standing close to each other, his eyes fell on her face, her pink glow maddened him, he took a step forward to her.

A wave of fear went down her spine and she started shivering. Marcus wrapped his arms around her waist, she raised her head and looked into his dark blue glittering eyes, he pulled her closer to him, "Olivia,"

A spark went down her spine when his cold minty breath falls on her face, her face heated up,

His dark blue eyes boring into her chocolaty brown eyes making her blush, the elevator stopped and with the jerk, he unwrapped his arms and she took a step back with a snap,

Both walked out of the elevator, and he took her to the room.

Marcus helps her sit on the bed, like a gentleman.

"Don't stress yourself, Olivia, you still need to rest, If you want something, then use this telecom," he said pointing towards a cordless phone placed on the bedside,

She submissively nodded,

"Are you hungry, Olivia?" he asked pouting as if he was starving,

Before she could answer him back, he took the telecom and ordered lunch for both,

After a while, two butlers entered the room with the trolley of lunch,

"Master your lunch", One of the butler's said politely and the other started serving them,

He offered Marcus a plate of red sauce pasta, "The lady first."

Marcus said giving the plate to Olivia,

Though Olivia is not very hungry, she still can't dare to refuse, she reluctantly takes the plate and took a spoon,

"I have the best cook in the world, they cook the most delicious food" Marcus praises his cook eating the food,

"Yes, I agreed," she said taking a spoon of pasta close to her mouth,

Both happily enjoyed the lunch together, It is the first time Marcus and Olivia are eating together sitting close to each other,

He keeps on stealing glances at her face and smirking.

 "What?" she frowned.

 He shoved his gaze, took a tissue paper, and gently wiped the red sauce from the corner of her lips,

"Eat comfortably, sugar candy"...he whispered in his ears, his breath once again fans her cheeks, she shrugs with him sitting so close to her,

She turned her head to ignore his gaze and finished her Pasta.

"I am done," she said hurriedly putting down her plate,

"Are you sure?" He curiously asked.

He also put down his plate and raised his hand to signal the butlers to take the stuff out of the room,

She looked at the washroom door, but hesitated to ask for permission,

"You can use your washroom, Olivia. It's your room now, you don't have to be hesitant," he gently said looking at her,

He can also read my gestures...that's great, she maliciously smiled thinking of both the brothers.

"Okay, I have to leave, see you tomorrow,"

"Tomorrow? Are you going somewhere, master?" she curiously asked batting her eyelids.

"Yes, actually we both are going out tonight and will be back by tomorrow, so be safe and manage yourself," he sounds dull.

He leaned on Olivia and softly kissed her forehead, "take care of yourself sugar candy" after bidding her goodbye, he walked out of the room.

She heaved a sigh and threw her back on the sofa with her arms supporting her head back.

Now both the wizard princes are so possessive about her that they forget their revenge and started feeling for her, this is what she wanted them to be like. Her plan has been perfectly executed so far. She succeeds in taming them.

Tonight, there will be a red moon in the sky, this is the night she is desperately waiting for.

Marcus and Arthur will be out of the palace tonight and she can easily look after what she has been implanted here,

Arthur came to Marcus to ask for tonight's plan,

"How can we leave her alone in the palace"? Arthur considerately asked.

"Don't worry about mom, she is safe in this palace, nobody can dare to enter in here. Whoever will come in without our consent will automatically be cursed, hope you remember that! Marcus affirmed that he is very confident with his security arrangements,

'How about Olivia?" Arthur abruptly asked Marcus heartbeat paces up with this question, but he can't trust anyone.

"Olivia??? how can you be doubtful about her, Arthur?" Marcus was shocked to hear Arthur,

"Arthur, you were the one, who always found her innocent now you are doubting her, why bro?" He asked looking into his eyes.

"When it comes to mom, I can't trust anyone?" his eyes filled with emotions,

"Olivia is a harmless girl to us, so you don't worry about her. I will make sure that mom will be safe tonight," Marcus said confidently as he always has an eye on Olivia through the CCTV.

"Arthur listen to me very carefully, the Red moon is coming after 500 years, this is our one-time golden opportunity to reverse the curse on our mom and we can't afford to fail," He strongly stated.

"We have to get her back," he patted Arthur's shoulder and tried to motivate him,

"What if we fail brother?" Arthur frightenedly asked.

"WE WILL WIN!" Marcus yelled at him

"Repeat after me Arthur, WE WILL WIN...we will win...we will win."

"Yes, we will win!" Arthur shouted in confidence

The room echoed with their words,

Olivia heard their screams, a vicious smile crept over her lips "yes you will win, you have to win for me tonight you poor twins!" she exclaimed to herself.

Both discuss their plans, on the other hand, the harmless Olivia has her own plans,

 She has her own purpose to be here. She has not been kidnapped. She approached them and helped them kidnapping her.

CHAPTER-17 "THE PARTICIPANTS"

Both the wizard princes met at the cliff during the crepuscular hours. Arthur was carrying his black cloak whereas Marcus had already put his cloak on him. Marcus raised his eyebrows looking at the nervousness spread over Arthur's face,

"Arthur..." he angrily yelled, Arthur snapped and immediately wore the cloak he was carrying in his hands and jumped down the valley, Marcus followed him and soon both disappeared in the air,

The valley is the secret door to the magical world and both landed in a coliseum. The ancient, enormous, really towering arena is massed with the magicians around the universe. All have gathered on the auspicious occasion of "The Red Moon".

The high-intensity floodlights around the arena made it look more illustrious, turning the darkness of night into a bright day. The mountains surrounded the arena making it more adventurous to be a part of this competition.

The chaos of wizards and witches of all the ages, all genders and all races are here, some are giant tall, some are minute wizards, some elderly wizards are addressing the mass,

Arthur and Marcus wandering down the arena and tried to find what would their next step be to move here.

Scene point of view

In the world of magic, the red moon appears in the sky after a particular time interval, but it has come after 500 years. On this auspicious day, the red moon empowered the winner with all the legendary powers of the wizards. Who so ever wins the cup will get the powers, The power given by the red moon can reverse any curse or spell even the forbidden killing spell, which is one of the irreversible spells in the wizards..

Arthur and Marcus came here to participate in this competition to win the cup so that they can reverse the curse on their mother. The goblet of fire randomly uses the participants. The names have already been put in the goblet by all the kingdoms ministers the week prior to this event. Today, the fire will come up with the selected participants' names.

An elderly wizard wearing a white cloak, having a snow-white long beard and puffed eyes with a wrinkled face flew over the arena on his broom. He landed in the middle of the ground on a huge stage made by cutting the huge rock, he stood there and grew taller and taller like a giant, everyone stood from their respective seats and bowed to him with respect. He is "The Lord of the magical World" and "Lord Reece Whitesman". His aura is so positive, that the young generation facing him for the first time in their lives is stunned to see his powerful appearance.

Arthur and Marcus's eyes glowered to see him personally, as they only read about him in the stories in the wizard school of magic.

"Welcome to the Magical world my children" he addresses everyone using his wand as the mic. His voice is clearly audible to the thousands of accumulated magicians,

"I, Lord Reece, came here to announce the name of the participants and I am very happy to have you all here," Immediately the Bowl of fire appeared in front of him and he rolled his wand over the fire, the smog erupted over the fire and shadow of a face appeared in that "Prince of sharks" the shadow yelled,

"Prince of Sharks" Lord Reece repeats. A group from the kingdom of sharks starting jumping in excitement and raised the Prince of Shark on their shoulders. Everyone applauded, then the Prince of sharks flew to Lord Reece and joined him on stage arrogantly waving at everyone. The prince of sharks is a handsome, muscular boy of around 25 years with green eyes and curly blonde hair, his white skin has small fins and gills on it.

Butterflies started floating in everyones stomach to know who will be the next. Every eye is desperately looking to the Bowl of fire.

"Princess of Pearls" the smog face yelled another name, on hearing that, A girly group started shouting in excitement and hugged their princess she turned into a pearl and flew to the stage.

All eyes turned to the 22 years old beautiful rose white princess, she is damn beautiful. She looked sizzling in her pink cloak, she has beautiful black eyes and long black wavy hair, her tall perfectly curved figure can stunt any man around. Everyone finds her fragile to be a participant in this hardcore competition, but no one can oppose the decision of the Bowl of fire.

She bowed to the Lord with respect and sweetly waving at the audience, each head again turned into the fire bowl.

Arthur and Marcus' heartbeats pace up, both looked into each other's eyes. On the one hand, Marcus is quite confident they will be definitely selected while Arthur, whereas on the other hand, Arthur is nervous about the event and their participation.

In this competition, only young generations of princes, and princesses of the magical world can participate and can win the competition showcasing their mental, physical and magical powers.

All the participants have prepared for long time and undergone very tough and thorough training before putting their names for participating.

Every eye excitedly turned back to the bowl of fire. Their eyes glowered in excitement. Few participants are afraid of the danger and few are forcefully came here. A mixture of expressions and feelings can be experienced here.

"Princes of Snakes" the smog loudly growled.

Arthur and Marcus froze on hearing their names, yes, they are the young generation of the kingdom of Snakes, everyone screamed looking at the twin prince on the stage with the Lord.

They are opposing the participation of the twins they want the game to be fairer and solo prince to participate,

"SILENCE."

Lord Reece frowned and yelled.

The screams turned into whispers, "it is a conspired!" "They fooled the fire bowl, the snakes are always hypocrites," many other whispers started spreading down the arena. It is obvious that the kingdom of snakes has more opponents than friends.

"For me, all my children are equal. Now, As the twin princes have been selected by the goblet itself nobody can oppose its decision. May the best and the most deserving participant win."

"Let's begin" ... colourful fireworks fired in the sky as the lord raised his wand in the air...

Everyone gets excited.

Chapter-18 "THE ULTIMATE WINNERS"

The competition is to walk down the magical maze to find the powerful victory cup to win.

Whoever will reaches the cup first will be considered as the ultimate winner. There is no rule for the participants to play, they can use any of their abilities, wizardly skills and strength. One thing while battling in the maze is you can't kill your opponent.

Four of the selected participants arrived at the entrance of the magical maze. They all are wearing a similar uniform black t-shirt and black track pants carrying their magic wands in their hands.

All look powerful and confident. The Prince of Sharks harshly glanced at all his opponents and arrogantly stand at the entrance, whereas the sweet princess cutely smiled looking at the others.

The twin brothers neutrally gaze all over.

"Are you ready, participants?" Lord Reece asked loud from the stage,

All the participants raised their wands and green lights flashed out simultaneously.

The participants moved to their respective assigned entry point and the competition begins,

All four ran in the maze,

The maze is made using moving magical bushes that keep on changing their positions, the maze is full of creepy creatures that can attack the participants from anywhere.

The participants have to be very alert all the time, their minor mistakes can lead them to lose the victory cup.

During the first stage, the pearl princess courageously running straight into the maze making way by shoving the bushes using her wand, Suddenly, a giant shark jumped over her and grabbed her neck, she didn't freak out, though cunningly and courageously used the frozen spell and the whale freezes in the same position, immediately the shark turned into the shark prince. Everyone thought her to be a weak, a naive contender to be attacked first and throw her out of the competition, and with the same thought prince of Sharks tried to push her out from the maze but his idea backfired on him and he got trapped in his web.

The princess slightly crawled down from the frozen Prince of Sharks and again started running forward looking for the way to the next stage of the maze.

She successfully crossed the first stage and entered the second stage. The frozen prince body disappeared into bushes and reached back into the arena.

Everyone present in the arena was shocked to see the strongest contender of the competition, come out so soon.

He blackouted and the minister started asking for medical assistance for him. The lord declared him disqualified.

In the maze, the Snakes princes bravely fought and won over the dragon lizards and entered the second stage running fast like a wolf straight in the bushes.

The second stage is more dangerous. They have to fight the big alligators, that are coming from everywhere, Arthur and Marcus attacked the alligators with the spell of fire as alligators are afraid of fire the twin brothers parted away from each other to fight the alligators. Arthur tried to distract the alligator and making ways for Marcus to jump into the door of the third stage.

They are playing really smart collaborating with each other with their snake hisses. Suddenly, the Pearl princess who was deliberately hiding in the bushes appeared and distracted Marcus by throwing a spell over him, he somehow defends the spell, The moment he tries to stabilize himself, the Pearl Princess ran straight towards the closing door and entered the third stage door, the brightly shining rose gold victory cup can be easily seen through the sliding door.

Marcus was about to take a step forward suddenly a big alligator grabs his leg and bites him hard. He groaned in pain and meticulously enchants a spell on the alligator and the alligator died. But, the Alligators severely injured him. Arthur looked at the injured Marcus, who was unable to stand on his feet.

Arthur enchanted a spell and his lowered body turned into a golden snake tail and he grew wings in his back, he actually turned into a flying snake.

He furiously flew over the alligator clench Marcus tightly in his hands and speedily flew in the narrow sliding door which was about to close. They successfully entered the third stage, the princess got scared looking at them flying high over and got distracted and fell into the pit of fire which she was about to jump.

She got a panic attack and fainted falling in the fire pit. Arthur flew down the pit and ordered Marcus to save her, Marcus Immediately grabs her hand.

Arthur flew over the victory cup that was plotted on a small rock, leaving behind all the hurdles. When they reached over the victory cup Marcus bent down and took the victory cup with his other hand.

Arthur flew out of the maze and landed in front of Lord Reece. Everyone jumped from their seats and was amazed to see Arthur holding Marcus and Marcus carrying Pearl Princess in his one hand and holding the rose gold victory cup in the other.

Marcus softly put down the unconscious Pearl Princess on the stage and Arthur got back onto his legs, his wings also disappeared. He also helped Marcus to sit carefully avoid hurting his legs. Arthur kneeled beside him; both raised the cup high in their hands.

Both have bruises and scratches all over their face and body, the bruises narrating the story of how courageously they fight backed the creepy hurdles inside the maze.

Arthur was overwhelmed with their win and hugged Marcus tightly gasping heavily. "WE WON Bro! We Won!" tears dribbled down his cheeks.

"You made us win Arthur," Marcus gently rubbed his back trying to calm him, he heaves a sigh.

Lord Reece signalled the doctor to help Marcus and the Pearl Princess.

"So, here we have the Winners 'The Princes of Snakes'," Lord growled happily addressing the audience. Everyone applauded in joy. Praise their presence of mind and wizardry skills. They use the right skills at the right time.

Everyone is starting to love them now, hatred from their hearts has gone out as they not only won the competition but didn't harm any of their contenders as others tried to do. Moreover, the Princes of snakes saved the Pearl Princess from falling into the pit of the fire.

Arthur and Marcus proudly holding the Victory cup. Emotions welled up in their eyes. Arthur saw his mother smiling in the cup whereas Marcus looks the cup as a sword to his revenge.

<u>CHAPTER-19 "THE QUEEN"</u>

The competition finished with the declaration of the winners. Everyone went back to their homelands.

The Lord took the ultimate winner princes to a secret door. The door opens with the lord's gesture.

The red sharp bright light appeared the prince couldn't bear the red glare and subconsciously raised his hands to block the glare pouring into their eyes. The room was filled with bright red moonlight and one huge Royal Golden Throne was situated in the middle of the room. Princes were amused to see the room.

The Lord entered the door and the twins obediently followed him.

"Put down the victory cup and your wands on that throne," Lord politely ordered the princes pointing his hands towards the golden throne.

The prince altogether holds the cup and softly put it on the golden throne and took a step back, A red flash poured into the cup from a big hole on the wall.

After a while the lord came forward and took the cup and poured out the red liquid in two golden glasses and handed it over to Arthur and Marcus.

"Have it, my boys, it is the holy and the most powerful liquid of the universe."

Both, looked down into the glasses, the blood-red liquid is emitting luminous flashes, a knot went down their throats, initially both hesitated and then later drank it in one go.

A red spark went down their veins, their bodies shook with the power and red light flashed out their blue iris as soon as they swallowed the complete drink. After a while both stabilized themselves and smiled looking at each other, feeling immensely powerful.

The Lord then handed them their wands back.

"You and your wands now have been empowered with the powers of the Red Moon; Now use these powers wisely my children." The Lord politely advised Arthur and Marcus.

"One thing Princes, you can use your powers only to protect and help others, only for the Good-wills. If you will use these any of your powers on anyone with any evil intentions the powers will be immediately taken back from you both", his voice is deep and harsh this time.

Both the boys nodded and bowed with respect and disappeared with a snap.

In the Smith Mansion, The moment Arthur and Marcus left the mansion, Olivia laid on the bed curved herself in the thin quilt pretending to be asleep. she slowly shrugged her head under the quilt and after a while a small red ant walked down the bed and hurriedly ran out of the door, The ant started moving to the private floor.

The ant kept walking and rolled down to the last door of the corridor, entered the room where the old lady was lying on the bed. After entering the room, the ant changed into Olivia.

Olivia was standing in front of the queen size bed looking at the old sleeping lady.

The old lady is Queen Vincent Smith, Queen of the Kingdom of snake and mother of the twin princes.

She is not sleepy she is paralysed because of the forbidden killing spell that shoot on the king of the snake she tried to save him and got affected by the spell, somehow, she survived but paralysed and slipped in a state of coma since then.

Marcus and Arthur blamed King Cox behind the attack and consider him the killer of their father and their mother of this condition, this is what they want Olivia to pay back them.

Olivia moved towards the head of the Queen, She raised her hand and bowed with respect,

"Hail the Queen,"

She flips her hand and a white, shining, bright pearl popped out of her palm. She took the pearl and slightly rolled the pearl over Queen temple, a bright light rolled over her head and Queen widely opened her eyes, as if she had woken up after long sleep.

Olivia's face brightens up, she excitedly bowed her again and shouted "Hail the Queen."

The queen rolled her eyes at Olivia and her eyes glowered looking at her.

The queen wanted to speak but couldn't speak her throat dried up. Olivia looks around the room and saw a jug of water at the center table.

She immediately moved to the table and grabbed the jug and poured some water into the glass. She hurriedly walked back to the bed and sat near Vincent's head, she supported her with one hand and slightly raised Vincent's head and slowly helped her sip some water to quench her thrust.

Vincent took a sip and slightly coughed as she drank water after 15 years. Olivia put the glass on the side table and wipes Vincent's face.

"I am glad to see you alive, Queen." Olivia's eyes welled up with emotion. Vincent still couldn't move her body but came out from the state of coma.

"Who are you girl?" Vincent shuttered

"Queen, I am Olivia, Princess of Kingdom crystal."

Hearing Kingdom crystal a tear rolled down by the side of Vincent's eyes.

"How is he?" she asked dryly.

"The king is saved and recovered well." Olivia sincerely answered.

"Queen it's been 15 years now."

"What???" Vincent was shocked to hear 15 years...

"Did I sleep for that long?" her words trembled, and she asked gasping in trauma

"Unfortunately, queen, it took 15 years for the second generation to grow and master the wizardry skills to fight back the dragons." Olivia sadly said lowering her head.

"I am happy that I reached you on time Queen. Tonight, is the Red Moon Night."

Vincent smirked and tears of happiness rolled out. "Were my boys able to win?"

"Yes, Queen, definitely they will win, and I am sure they tried their level best to win."

Olivia heard the footsteps.

"They are back queen; I have to go. I will see you soon, you take care." She bowed with respect again.

Olivia hurriedly turned back in an ant and rolled out of the door.

The queen again closed her eyes.

Chapter-20 "BROTHERHOOD"

Arthur and Marcus' pacing towards their mom's room.

Olivia turned into an ant again slowly walking out of the room and through her tiny ant eyes, she saw both the boys coming to her.

Through her ant eyes, the boys look like giants reaching her, she slowly crawling by the wall fearing of not getting crush under their feet.

Arthur was smiling lost in his own thoughts of happiness and satisfaction. "Mom will be proud of me and will soon wake up. I will never let her down and soon may be introduced Olivia to her" Marcus busy fascinating about his small happy moments with his Oliv.

Marcus who is walking beside with the same pace is also busy in his own thoughts with an arrogant smile on his lips.

"Mom and Dad both will be proud of me; I just wish mom to wake up soon and reveal the deepest darkest secret of our lives."

Suddenly. he paused and looked around..." Olivia" he murmured...he can sense her; this is the same moment when the ant and Marcus crossed each other.

Arthur who was almost 10 steps ahead of him by now, realised that he was walking alone he stopped and turned back,

"Marcus"

Marcus snapped and fluttered..." yeah coming bro"... he replied.

He took long steps to reach Arthur. He kept looking here and there.

"What happened bro, you look lost?"

Arthur concernedly asked.

"Nothing, I felt Olivia around!"...he exclaimed perplexedly looking back in the long corridor, the tension in his thoughts can easily be detected from his face.

"What?" Arthur unbelievably yelled and looked back following Marcus gaze,

"No one is there, bro"...he giggled.

Marcus sighed and patted Arthur's shoulder.

"Let's meet mom, I think I am tired and hallucinating her. I need to rest." He immediately unlocked the door and both entered with winning smiles on their faces.

Soon, Olivia disguise as an ant reached her room.

On the other hand, the queen closed her eyes as she can't reveal that she is out of the coma to her kids. It's not the right time for her to wake up,

Whereas, Olivia was quite nervous as if how queen will behave in front of the boys, she couldn't get much time to explain to Vincent about the current scenario,

"Please god of magic please save us," She prayed to turn back into Olivia's figure.

She is the queen though she was in a state of coma but don't forget she is also a wizard queen my friends.

She was in continuous telepathy connections with the outer world with her love and loved ones.

She calmly closed her eyes and pretended to be in a state of coma,

Both the boys reached their moms and excitedly shouted like small kids...

"WE WON MOM," Marcus kneels down beside her bed and emotions welled up in his eyes looking at his mom calm and emotionless face.

"Please Mom wake up now, I have a lot to share with you mom, please" he started sobbing holding Vincent's hand kissing the back of her hand,

Arthur knelt down beside Marcus and rubbed his back and tried to calm him down.

"Don't worry bro, Mom will soon wake up", he was trying hard to push his tears back while consoling his elder brother, Marcus immediately turned back and hugged Arthur tightly and cried loudly,

"How long we have been waiting for mom to wake up, Arthur? Now no more patience left in me," He is gasping crying loud.

Arthur kept staring at Vincent's face with watery eyes, his hands kept rubbing at Marcus's back.

"Soon bro, soon!" Arthur's sound deep and confident.

Arthur pulled back from his shoulders and tried to calm him down,

"We should celebrate our victory, what say bro?" Arthur said smilingly. Marcus smiled back wiping his tears with his palms like a small boy.

Both stood firmly and looked at their mom's face and smiled..."We love you, mom." They said simultaneously.

Both kissed her on the forehead one by one and went out of the room. They reached Marcus room...

Marcus strolls towards the small bar in his room and pulled out his favourite scotch bottle from the cabinet with two glasses in his hand and reached Arthur who is calming shrugging on the sofa dreaming of Oliv...

"Hey, little one why are you blushing?" Marcus chuckled pouring the scotch into glasses.

Arthur was caught off guard, Arthur snapped out of his thoughts and shyly looked at Marcus, "Nothing bro,..I was thinking of our future" he flustered.

"OUR?" Marcus' eyes widened looking at Arthur face like a big question mark flashed in his eyes.

"You and me,...our...hmm our..." he huffs winking and sneered taking the one glass from the table and raising a toast he shouted "cheers to our victory bro"... "cheers," Marcus smiled and their glasses slightly touched and made a ting sound and both took their scotch in one go.

"You played well tonight, Arthur!" Marcus exclaimed wiping his mouth and his eyes sparkled with joy.

"You too bro!"...Arthur stood and leaned on Marcus and hugged him tightly.

"You owe me, Arthur, you saved me today, I am sitting in front of you healthy and alive because of you, just because of you!" he again poured scotch in both of the glasses and back-to-back had both the glasses,

Both kept talking about their experiences and feeling while playing their parts in the maze, the rest of the night is mixtures of emotions and giggles echoed in the room and both drank till the dawn and passed out on each other like chuddy buddy.

After their parents were attacked, they both helped each other to grow, both have shared so much good and bad altogether, though both have their own point of view with respect to their style of living and attribute towards their goal.

They share a strong bond as twins. Marcus is arrogant and rude whereas Arthur is humble and grounded.

Both have their souls and lives joined, sleeping deep in each other arms, enjoying Brotherhood.

Chapter-21 "THE LOST KINGDOM"

A tear rolled out from the corners of Vincent's eyes as she saw her kids after so many years, unfortunately, she couldn't reveal in front of them that she came out of the coma.

She was happy to see her sons together taking care of each other...thinking of what she missed in her life.

She trails down the memory lane with tears streaming down her cheeks.

*16 years ago in the Smith palace

The king and the queen were happily having tea and snacks in the palace garden with their two little children playing football around.

"Kids come here first, finish your milk," Vincent called Arthur and Marcus.

Arthur and Marcus replied in unison turning back to their parents, "Coming Mom."

The two little princes having blue sparkling eyes and sweet innocent smiles on their faces came running to their parents.

"Have your snacks and then you can go back to play," Vincent said rubbing Arthur's hair.

Whereas Marcus runs his fingers in his hair and sits next to his dad, King Richard Smith smiles at him rubs Marcus back with love in his eyes and gestures to Marcus to eat his food.

"Dad when will you go on a vacation? It's been so long we haven't gone out." Marcus asked with his half-filled mouth.

"Soon, my child!" King-Smith said sighing.

Those days Kingdon dragon was attacking the magic world, killed many wizards kings, their families and forcefully captured their kingdoms. Therefore, to ensure the securities of the rest of the magical kingdoms the ministry of magic summoned every wizard king and instructed them not to leave their palaces and kingdoms until the situation is under control.

Kingdom of Snakes and Crystal Kingdom was in a friendly relation as King Cox and King-Smith were best friends. They always said that when their kids grow up they will turn their friendly relations into family relations by getting them married their kids to each other.

By that time no one ever thought of the danger coming their way.

After almost 6 months everything has changed, Dragons are now everywhere numerous wizards kingdoms were captured by Dragons who don't join hands with the dragons ended up in graves.

King Cox and King-Smith were worried about their families as well and always searching for a way to fight back dragons and to defeat them. As, they are one of the strongest Kings of the magic world, dragons didn't dare to attack them earlier,

The dragons King was very cunning, cruel and heartless. He is empowered with all the evil powers.

He never let others live happily. His evil desire is to conquer the whole magical world by hook or crook.

One day King Cox suddenly came to visit King-Smith.

A fair, tall, well-toned muscular man wearing a black cloak having an ear to ear smile on his face entered the Smith palace.

"Hey Richie, my friend! "...he stretches his arms wide for King-Smith to hug, King-Smith, who was having lunch with his family, was surprised to hear his voice and turned his side to look at him.

"Oh my god!" His eyes sparkled with happiness,

"I can't believe I am seeing you, Henry." He stood up from his chair and walked to his childhood friend King Henry Cox hugged him tightly feeling his embrace.

Every one-stopped eating and turned to them,.."Hey, kids see who came to visit us?" his words are filled with happiness.

Queen Vincent welcomed him,

"Hello Henry, how are you? Good to see you after so long." she gave him a side hug,

"I am fine sis, how are you guys doing?"

Henry has no sister and when Richard started dating Vincent, they three used to spend a good time, since then Henry treated Vincent as his sister, they share a sweet and warm bond,

"Hello uncle," Princes bowed him with respect in unison.

"Hey kids, "Henry lean down and gave both the boys a warm hug and kissed their foreheads,

"God bless you, my children," both the kids ran out of the dining room to play.

"Come, Let's have lunch." Vincent smilingly gestures him to the dining table.

"I love to taste the food sister, but sorry to say I have a purpose to visit Richard." He sounds serious and nervous this time,

Her heart skips a beat hearing his words and she worriedly looked at Richard. He winks at her trying to make her calm.

King-Smith understood Henry nervousness as he called him Richard, which Henry only called when he has something serious to talk about,

"Oh, no worries Henry, Let us go to my study," Richard smiled and put his hand on Henry's shoulder and started walking upstairs,

"Honey, Henry definitely loved to have coffee made by you." Richard sneered looking above his shoulder walking beside Henry.

"I am sorry bro, I disturbed you in between your lunch,". Henry dryly apologizes for his surprise cum shock visit to his friend.

"Please bro, don't apologize! Anything for you Henry!" Richard exclaimed rubbing Henry's back with his left hand.

"Thanks, bro!" Henry nervously runs his hand in his hair.

Both entered the study...

"Have a seat," Richard grabbed a chair for Henry and sits in front of him.

"What happened Henry? why are you tensed? Is everything fine there in Crystal palace?" He bombarded so many questions at Henry as Richard never saw his joyfully and humorous friend like this ever before.

He was also aware of the danger swinging like a sword on both the kingdoms but he knows well that Henry is one of the strongest and powerful wizards and won over so many evil powers...his fear grew more and more, his heart is beating faster by now,

Henry collected his words and tried to explain what was going on in his head and heart.

They saw Vincent trailing in the study carrying a tray with two cups of coffee and chicken sandwiches for them.

"Sorry to disturb you guys, hope you enjoy talking with some homemade food," Vincent said placing the tray on the small center table in front of them...

"Thanks, honey." Richard smiled.

"I wish you would have brought my dolls and Lily with you, Henry, so that I could also get a chance to meet my friend, my princes were also missing their princesses," Vincent chuckled handing the cup of coffee to Henry.

"Next time for sure sister," Henry replied calmly taking the cup of coffee from her,

Vincent senses the nervousness of the situation and asked for the leave, "Ok, guys you enjoy."

"Vincent...," Henry grabbed her by the arm as she was about to move away,

Hearing her name from his mouth after years a tear of sadness rolled down her cheeks, she pushed her emotions back and wiped her tear with another hand and turned 180 degrees at him, now she understood why he is here all of a sudden.

"I want you to stay as well," Henry said putting back his cup on the table Vincent took a chair next to him.

Henry heaved a sigh out and started telling why he came?

"As we all know King Dragon has become the most powerful evil wizard king, we all can't defend him likewise, many kingdoms have been ruined by his attacks, moreover the ministry of magic failed to negotiate with him, hundreds of wizards lost their lives, dragons captured their kingdoms empowering Dragons territories. Evidently, dragons are still not satisfied.

"I am afraid to say this, now they are behind the FOUR CRYSTALS OF MAGIC."

"What??" Vincent's eyes widened and she jumped off the chair in shock,

Richard moved to her and tried to calm her, "Calm down Honey, let him complete,"

He made her sit again and held her hand tightly taking a chair next to her.

"Sorry dear, I tried to handle it for long time, but now I am also feeling helpless in front of the immensely powerful dragons," Henry said holding his head in his hand as if he is totally tired.

"I came here to seek a favor from you both." Henry sadly asked for a favor.

CHAPTER -22 "PAST"

Richard slightly leaned over to Henry and pressed his shoulder to console and strengthen him,

"Henry, my friend, I am always there for you, irrespective of the danger we all are in."

Vincent also joined Richard and courageously held Henry's hand tightly.

"We are with you brother!"...She composedly exclaimed.

Richard winks at her with a warm smile.

Henry took out a golden box from his cloak pocket and handed it to Vincent,

Vincent surprisingly looked at the box, "What is it in this box brother?" She curiously asked looking at the box, she was about to open the box when Richard stopped her.

"NO! Don't open," Vincent jerked with his sudden harsh voice.

Vincent, this box has our lives and freedom of our next generations, Henry seriously said.

"You are being the crystal heiress, you know where exactly to hide this box?"

Vincent wondering what is he saying?

Richard continued as Henry voice was filled with emotions and he failed to speak more.

"Honey, you know! What dragons are afraid of?"

"Yes, we all know, She abruptly answered... "Wo." She was about to say the place.

"Shhh." Henry put his finger on Vincent's lips and signalled her not to speak further.

Vincent was unable to understand what they both were up to.

"Vincent just keep it with you and just keep this box at a safe place."

"I regret to say you need to swear the secretary...Swear?" Vincent cut him off in the middle and looked shockingly at Richard,

"Dragons have their invisible spies everywhere maybe some are here also."

Vincent trembled to look here and there around the room, "Here in this room?" She fearfully mumbled looking at Henry.

"No, not in this room honey, you know Dragons can't sneak in Snake kingdom," Richard said.

She sighed in relief,

Henry stood from his chair and with watery eyes, he speaks out his emotions "I don't have much time friends, maybe it's our last meeting."... Vincent and Richard jumped out of their chair and stood by Henry's side.

"Dragons are coming to us, Richard you be careful," He shuttered and hugged Richard tightly as if he will never get a chance to meet him again,

And, then he turns to Vincent hugs her tightly, "Take care of this box, only this box is our last hope, Sis..." Vincent burst out into tears,

Richard steps forward and holds Vincent by her shoulder looking at Henry with watery eyes. "Take care, my friend,"

"I failed to save my people, but I will never let you down," with this Henry disappeared.

Vincent fell on her knees and cried out loudly holding the golden box tightly close to her chest.

"Don't go please...don't..." She screams crying out loudly...Richard held her tightly in his arms.

Richard being a man can't even show up his pain, he somehow controls his tears and tried calming Vincent.

"Vincent, look into my eyes," He said cupping her face in his hand and forcing her to stop crying.

Vincent submissively looked into his eyes.

His dark blue eyes which are always calm and pour love on her are now pouring courage,

"Vincent..., he gave you a responsibility to save our next generation, You can't let our brother, our only friend and our future family let down. You and only you can save both the kingdoms."

Vincent tried hard to calm down.

"How?" She asked sobbing,

"Go to the place where you love to spend most of your time and you will get all the answers, today is the full moon."

 "You will get all your answers. 'Under the yellow moonlight in the blue ambience with a golden companion'." He riddles it out.

Vincent understood the riddle and stood firmly wiping her tears.

"I will never let anyone of us down." She ran out of the room,

The kids who were playing in the corridor saw their mom crying, running out of the room they thought King Cox hurt her.

They were just 10 years old and were unable to understand the irony of time...

Arthur and Marcus ran behind calling her again and again...

"Mom"

"Mommy...stop."

But, she ignored her kids and ran to her room and closed the door,

She leaned back on the door crying and sobbing...She slides down besides the door and clenched her knees to her chest digging her head in her knees sobbing more and more.

She was crying because of the thought that, Henry and his family will be soon killed by the dragons. Henry came here to save them even in such a critical situation.

He could have saved his family but he chose us over his family, this is how a true and honest friend behaves, she was surprised and shocked at the same time.

"Henry, you fulfilled your promise as a brother, you always promised me to save me and my family, and today in the time of need you came up to save us."

She cried aloud saying, "I love you, bro we all love your bro, I will miss you all, I love you, Lily, I wish I could also see you all the last time, Oli and Ze.."

"Mom...please open the door," Arthur shouted from behind the door knocking hard on the door,

Vincent came out of her trance and wiped her tears put the box in the cupboard,

Opened the door faking a smile.

"What happened, Arthur? She started looking at him...

He hugged her tightly... "Mom, why were you crying?" He innocently asked..."Did King Cox hurt you?"

"No, my son, your uncle can never hurt any of us. I cried because he visited us for a while, I want him to stay longer," She lied faking a smile.

"Then, why are you crying now?" He innocently asked wiping a tear that was rolling down her cheeks.

"Just emotions Arthur, always remember my words Arthur, Crystal Kingdom and Uncle Cox never hurt us in fact we owe them many things, we owe them our lives too," She said rubbing her fingers in his hair.

"Mom, don't do that!" he frowned and ran back to Marcus who was still playing calmly in the corridor.

CHAPTER-23 "PRESENT"

End of the flashback

In Marcus's room

Arthur woke up with his mobile's ringing, which was lying on the floor as last night both the brothers had celebrated their victory and they drank well till dawn, they danced, laughed and enjoyed.

In that heat of enjoyment, his cell phone might have fallen out of his pocket which he didn't realise at that moment.

He woke up leaning his head on the headboard of the bed. He looked around rubbing his eyes for his phone and forcefully opened his eye as he found himself in Marcus's room. Recalling the events of the last night. He jumped off the bed when his phone rang again,

He looked here and there with his one

Hand on his waist and running his other hand's finger in his hair.

He saw his cell phone lying on the floor under a cushion. He immediately answered the phone and frowned to hear what the caller said., His heart actually skips a few heartbeats. He palmed his mouth in shock and took a deep breath before continuing.
"Ok, I will be there in a moment."

"What happened, Arthur?" Marcus who also woke up with Arthur's cell phone ringtone groggily asked

Marcus yawned, dizzily looking at Arthur with sleepy eyes. "Oh...Nothing serious bro! I have two scheduled surgeries in the afternoon and need to discuss the procedure with my medical team, it was a reminder call." He shuttered and left the room. "See you later bro." Arthur left waving his hand in the air.

Marcus also came out of the bed and walked to his bathroom. Arthur was stunned to know what his assistant doctor Jane said to him on the call.

"Damn! I knew it ...I knew." He said he was running his fingers in hair while pacing up to his mom's room, His eyes glowered with each step he takes towards the room. He stabilises his heart before entering the room. His heartbeat paced up fascinating the coming moments. He sighed looking at his mom face who is lying still on her bed. He kept staring at her taking a seat beside her and holds her lifeless hand in his.

"Mom, don't you feel like talking to your Arthur? Don't you want to see your son? Don't you mom? He paused and a drop of tear from his eyes fall on Vincent's hand and her eyelids flicked slightly. He noticed her reaction and continued speaking glancing at Vincent's facial reactions without blinking.

"Mom I know you can feel me, you can hear me and...
I also know that you are...AWAKE!" His words expressed his pain With his agonist words, Vincent couldn't control her emotions anymore and opened her eyes.

Arthur stood in shock and dropped her hand...tears of happiness started rolling out of his eyes... he ran his hand in his hair and rubbed his face. He couldn't believe his eyes. He immediately sat down beside her head and overwhelmingly kissed her head and cheeks.

"Mom, I knew it ...I knew that you are out of the coma, why didn't you tell us before? Mom?"

"Let me call Marcus, he will surely be on cloud nine with this good news.

He hurriedly took out his phone from his pocket and was about to dial Marcus. "Stop Arthur.!" Vincent slightly growled. Arthur dropped his phone with her voice.

"Mom..." tears of love and joy kept rolling out from his eyes. He hugged her leaning his half body on her and excitedly took the remote and elevated the head of the bed, Now, Vincent came in a half-sitting position, emotions welled up in her eyes too, as she saw her beloved son after long fifteen years.

"Oh, my son...I can't explain how happy I am to see you grown so well, you look as handsome as Richie," and she cried loud thinking of how she was parted from her family with a dragons attack.

.

Although she is awake, her body has not yet overcome from paralysis attack, The forbidden curse is yet to be reversed by her twin son in unison.

Arthur wrapped his arms around her shoulder and caressed her hand, "Mom now everything will be fine soon...
Mom, why did you stop calling me Marcus?" "Son, I am dying to see Marcus as well but the situation is still not in our control, we have to be careful with our each and every move." She sadly explained the critical situation.
"What do you mean by this mom?" Arthur anxiously interrupted her.
She coughed ...

Last night flashback

When Marcus was crying in Arthur's arms desperately wanted his mother to wake up. Arthur noticed that Vincent eye retina is moving under the eyelids as he is an experienced medical practitioner, he understood it at that time, that his mom is already out of the coma, and consoled Marcus saying that mom will soon awake. He was in a state of dilemma at that time about why mom is not showing up even though she is awake.

And, today held an hour ago

Arthur answered the call and Doctor Jane informed him that there are signs on the monitor that Queen is recovering from a coma maybe she is out of the coma, she wants Arthur to come and check his mom reports.

As, he was not sure that Mom was out of a coma or not, he didn't reveal that to Marcus and lied to him before leaving his room.

End of flashback.

Vincent coughed again, Arthur came out of his trance with her coughing and took a glass of water from the side table and helped, Vincent, to sip.

"Mom, why are you still afraid of anything? It's been fifteen years mom, now everything has changed, no dragons are there now." He tried calming her.

"Son..., only the time has changed not the dragons." She frowned.

"What?" Arthur widened his eyes and looked at Vincent's face as if she had grown horns.

CHAPTER -24 "FEAR"

Arthur was shocked to hear that the dragons still exist and desperate to capture their kingdom.

"But, Mom it's been 15 years now. We hadn't been any attack or haven't seen any dragon around us," he frantically said holding Vincent hand tightly looking into her eyes.

"Son, Dragon king was also badly injured that night, might be in the same condition as I am, he is such a manipulative and vicious man that he inherited the greed to become the world's powerful magician to his son,

Now, as his son has also grownup and maybe of your age, he sooner or later will definitely attack us."

"As only I know how to activate the diamond crystal one of the most powerful crystal kingdoms in the world of magic, I am not scared as I have my four crystals with me." she smirks saying her last sentence.

He nervously runs his hand in his hair and sweat beads up on Arthur's forehead.

"Mom, please let me summon Marcus, he is yearning for revenge with the Cox, and you know." He paused before completing his sentence. He thought he should not tell her right now that Marcus has kidnapped Olivia and assaulted her, Mom is very week and couldn't bear this news.

"Arthur just wait for the right time, I will explain everything clearly to both of you, day after tomorrow when your powers will be completely in control, and you both will reverse the curse on me. Everything will be sorted by then. Just be patient for one more day my son, I know it is very difficult for you to hide this from Marcus, but son the danger is everywhere, that is why you can't trust anyone." her eyes fledged again with the memory of past.

Mom, Marcus has waited for you to wake up, he cried much last night when we came back winning, please let me call him." his words are full of sadness.

"I am sorry son,"

"Mom, Uncle Jacob has raised us both very well, he was also praying every second for your wellness at least let me call him...Please, mom." he pleaded.

"NO..." she groaned.

"Try and understand Arthur as I told you danger is everywhere and we can't trust anyone, not even Jacob"...she is anxious.

Jacob used to be the most loyal Man of Richard, but you know he is the one who ditched us and let the Dragon army invade the kingdom and attack your father...

"Uncle Jacob? What are you saying, mom?" Arthur was in tremendous shock, he dropped her hand and immediately stood on his feet, looked at Vincent in disbelief.

"Mom, how come, Jacob?" he anxiously kept looking at her.

Arthur, I will explain to you everything later, for now, you just keep my secret with you...

Arthur didn't understand much of her words and nodded in a state of dilemma,

"Ok, mom, I trust you as you say...You should rest mom." He said pressing the remote button and turned the bed to its same position,

"Mom, I am so happy to have you back, nothing more matters to me other than you. I will surely keep your secret until you don't want to relieve it."

135

"I and Marcus missed you a lot, mom, we love you Mom...we love mom", his sentiments rolling out of his eyes,

" I love you too son..." she sneered with wet eyes.

CHAPTER-25 "DATE"

Olivia confusedly looks at the dress in her hand and sighed resting her back to the wall as from Marcus's calm behavior she concludes that so far, he is unaware of his mom condition. She stripped of what she is wearing and put on the maroon sleeveless, V- necked, body-hugging dress, brushed her red wavy hair and let them remain open,

"Looking wonderful in maroon color" she self-praised her looking in the mirror,

"Yes, you do look wonderful"... a husky sound came from beside...

She turned at the voice, it was Arthur who was standing with his arms close to his chest. She winked with surprise.

"Hey, Arthur, so good to see you, where were you?" she smirked asking.

His eyes sparkled looking at the gorgeous girl standing in front of him asking a question like a caring friend.

"Well, I was busy with a few patients," he said shyly rubbing his hair.

Olivia took a pair of matching wedges and put them on and pout looking in the mirror after applying maroon lip gloss...

"Hey, I asked you, I don't like latecomers and you..." Marcus entered the room scowling at Olivia and paused to see Arthur standing beside her...Arthur snapped with his voice and turned to him whereas Olivia trembles with his scowl...

"Are you guys going somewhere?" Arthur frantically asked rolling his eyes at both...

"Yeah, I am taking Oliv for a date" Marcus smirked winking at Arthur and stepped forward to entangle Olivia's hand in his and both walked out the room, Olivia embarrassedly looked at Arthur...

Arthur stood there shocked for a couple of minutes and came out of his trance of shock with Charity's voice who is here to clean the room,

 "Excuse me Master are you looking for something?"

"Aa...eh..NO," Arthur walked out of the room running his hand in his hair, burning in anger,

"'No, Marcus can't do that to me, he bought her here to assault her, to take his revenge now when I started feeling for her, he can't snatch her from me. No, he can't!" he frowned punching the wall,

Marcus took Olivia near the lake and there is a beautiful set up for them a round table with two chair under a big tree covered with yellow flowers, yellow flower petals were scattered all around on the ground and petals are showering from the tree branches with the breeze, Olivia mesmerized with the setup and the view, it's like her dream date, no one around only nature at its best...

Her eyes glittered with the thought of a date, she slightly pinched her palm as if she is dreaming,

Marcus turned to her, Olivia,... "I am trying to compensate for what I have done you?" He whispered in her ear...

Olivia looked at him, he actually seems to be some other Marcus, he was not the one who drugged her, raped her, not the one who pushed her out of the window, not the one who almost choked her to death, not who ...

Marcus leaned a little on her kissed her softly, she snapped with the sudden kiss, she was about to fall as he deepens the kiss, he immediately held her waist and tightly clenched her body closed to him intensely kissing her, this time there is no lust, no anger, it was a touch full of love and care,

Olivia can feel the difference, and also embraced the kiss with his divine smell,

"Mmm..." she moans as his tongue entangles her in her mouth, after a long kiss she pushed him away to have some air, panting heavily, both were looking into each other's eyes panting. her chest was heaving up and down faster.

He held her from the waist and gestured her to move to the table.

There was a wine bottle with two glasses and some delicious food.

He grabbed a chair for her like a gentleman and sat on the opposite side of the table in front of her...

He kept looking into her eyes, she shyly lowered down her head fidgeting with her fingers and biting her lower lip,

He took the wine bottle, opened it and poured the wine in two glasses handing over the one to Olivia and taking the other, "let's raise a toast for our new friendship journey," he smirked raising his hand for cheers.

"Yeah, Olivia nervously raises her hand"...cheers both sneered in unison and laughter burst out in the air,

"So, are you still afraid of me Olivia," he asked in a serious tone while sipping his wine.

"Er... actually Master, I am..." she stammers as she doesn't know what to answer.

"You can call me Marcus..." he smirked looking at her nervous face.

She widened her eyes hearing his husky breathtaking voice,

What the hell this prince want from me? His husky voice and divine smell making me mad, I want him inside me right away, Olivia thought in her head,

She rubbed the back of her neck in nervousness as her body got heated with her horny thought,

She gulped the wine to chill her heating sex hormones.

He does notice the change in her, her face turns red, and she often blushes, stealing glances at him,

Before Olivia could think of his next move, he took her in his arms like a new bride and put her on the flower bed, Marcus sat beside her, then turning her body towards him, he pulled her into him, their faces are just an inch away from each other! He looked into her eyes and then her lips.

She did feel his warm breath fans her face, "Marcus" a whisper left her mouth.

"Oliv!" Marcus whispered back. They kept staring at each other for a moment and then he brushed his lips on her soft lips very gently and whispered again, "Do you forgive me Oliv?" "I want the truth, a fearless honest answer!"

He didn't deepen the kiss, instead, he kept brushing his lips on her face, nose cheeks and slowly moving down her neck. his hands that were holding her moved to her waist brushing her skin through the fabric. He pressed his lips softly on her neck and she hung her head back arching like a bow, with her eyes closed in pleasure.

"Did you forgive me Oliv?" Marcus nibbled her skin and kept asking.

She could only breathe heavily as an electrifying feeling rose from her neck and spread all over her body. She wonders how he knows how to give her pleasure in such an away after brutally assaulting her,

Marcus rolled his hand at her back and started unzipping her dress,

Suddenly she has a flashback of his devilish assault, and a fearful shiver ran down her spine, she snaps and pushed him away... "No, I can't forgive you, No." she screamed in fear.

Marcus couldn't understand what happened to her, he tried to hug her embraced her to calm her, but she crawled slightly and ran away from the woods crying and furiously ran to her room.

"I have to go, I will see you soon mom." He left the room wiping his tears.

He was so overwhelmed with his mother's improving health.

On the other hand, Marcus came out of his washroom after completing his morning business.

Put an off-white v neck t-shirt and brown slim fit trousers, brushed his hair backwards, blushing looking into the mirror thinking of Olivia.

He took day off from office today and instructed Fin to handle all the meetings and not to call him unless it is not urgent.

He throws the brush on the table, swipes his mobile and goes of the room.

He went to the elevator and pressed the ground floor button as he was going to his dining room, suddenly an idea stuck in his mind and he pressed another floor button, the elevator stopped, and he walked out smirking and entered Olivia's room.

Oliva was standing beside the window lost in her thoughts.

"Thinking of me?" he chuckled in her ears.

She jerked with his sudden voice so close to her...

She looked at him and lowered her head fidgeting with the hem of her dress...

"Eh...Good...Good Morning Master..." she jittered.

"Good morning honey". He gave a peck on her cheek, and she blushed.

"So, how are you doing Olivia?" he asked grabbing her hand and she trembled in fear.

"I am good thank you for asking, master." Olivia replied lowering her head.

She is behaving so submissively, that Marcus couldn't control his emotions, he wanted to hug her, kiss her, embrace her...you can say he is completely mad at her now.

"Would you like to go for a date with me Olivia?" He said raising his hand towards her.

Olivia raised her head in shock and widened her eyes.

He furrows his brows at her, "What, why are you giving that shocking look?" "Am I looking like a ghost? " She stood frozen at her place.

"Hello... I am talking to you Olivia." he waved his hand in front of her face, she snaps,

"What did you just say, Master?" she winks at him thrice and pink dust covered her cheeks.

"Will you go on a date with me Ms. Olivia?" he said in a husky voice leaning close to her ears.

His minty breath fans her face and she felt a spark running down her veins, her arteries, to every inch of her body. She slightly turned on but somehow managed to control her horny avatar.

She curled her lips and stealing a glance at him.

He is looking, damn hot today in his casuals, she thought,

She is quite confused whether to say yes or no... before she could conclude what to answer. He opened her closet and selected a maroon sleeveless body-hugging dress for her and handed her the dress.

"Go get changed we will leave in half an hour." he sneered and landed a soft kiss on her pink lips.

Before she could understand what it's all about? he screamed going out of the room, "I don't like late fellows.

CHAPTER-26 "KINGDOM CRYSTAL"

Marcus was astonished by the sudden change in her reaction, for a moment he felt she forgive him and the next she ran refusing him.

Olivia directly ran into the bathroom and soaked herself in the bathtub filled with cold water just to chill her horny desires. After her body calms down, she thought of the mission she is on. "You can't fall in love Olivia you are on a mission; I have to accomplish my mission at the earliest." she kept murmuring to herself. She came out of the bathtub, dried herself and put on the cotton midi just to relax so that she can plan.

She came out of the room and looked around the room, heaving a sigh as she sat on the bed, resting her head on the headboard.

She jerked with a knock at the door, she thought it would be Marcus,

She couldn't find a way to hide from him, "What to do? What to do?" she murmured pacing in the room...Someone unlocked the door from outside and Olivia tightly closed her eyes in fear...

"Hey, Olivia..."

Oh, Alice, Olivia sighed taking Alice in her arms...

Marcus also came back to the mansion instead of confronting Olivia again, he directly walked to Arthur in his clinic...

"Arthur, I need to talk..." he sneered fidgeting with his mobile in his hand...

"Hi Bro...what a pleasant surprise, welcome to my clinic..."

Arthur stood from his chair and greeted Marcus,

"Have a seat bro"... Arthur ordered two cups of coffee for them...

"So bro How's your date with Olivia?" Arthur asked smirking...

"Disastrous..." he growled stamping his hand on the table...

Arthur was so happy to hear that but pretended to be sad in front of Marcus,

"Brother, I think Olivia is not your type of girl. You deserve someone better than her..." He said consoling Marcus...

"Arthur, I came here to discuss something serious than my date... he said grinning his teeth...

"Tell me, brother..."

Uncle Jacob called to inform me that he is coming back by tomorrow. Marcus informed Arthur...

"Really, Brother... One thing more brother tomorrow morning before dawn, we need to reverse the curse on mom...Arthur said cutting off Marcus

"Yes, I remember what Lord Reece told us..." Marcus said looking at his phone.

"Ok, Arthur, I have an important email to reply to... I will see you at dinner..." Marcus went out scrolling his phone.

The day went calm, Both the princes were busy with their works and Olivia was busy planning and plotting.

The next morning before dawn, Arthur and Marcus walked straight to Vincent's room.

"MOM..." Arthur called her but Vincent didn't move a bit...

Marcus looked at Arthur, "let us do it..." he signalled Arthur...

Both took out their red wands and started moving them in sync from Vincent head to toe enchanting a spell in unison. Arthur and Marcus were standing on either side of the bed.

A red flash of light started rolling down her body...

She trembles and opens her eyes wide with a jerk...

Mom... Marcus overwhelmed...

She took a deep breath and tried to move her hands then her feet...

"Yes Mom, you can do it"...Arthur cheered Vincent to try more...

Marcus's eyes sparkled to see Vincent moving he sit beside her and both the boys helped her to sit...

Mom, I can't tell how happy I am today, I have waited for fifteen years for you to come back mom, I missed you so much mom, Marcus cried hugging Vincent tightly, tears burst out from her eyes too...

Arthur also hugged her from the other side and kissed her hair.

"I am proud of you my sons..." Vincent said sobbing in Marcus's arms.

"Mom, please don't cry, Now everything will be fine... You are awake, me and Arthur won the Red Moon Powers, everything will be fine soon..." Marcus said wiping her tears with his hands.

Ameen, Arthur sneered.

Marcus listens to me son, I want you to know something very important, Vincent said holding Marcus hand in hers.

"What mom?..."

"A piece of information about your dad."

"Dad? I know mom, I saw how Cox attacked dad and killed him." He chuckled and his eyes filled with anger.

"No, Marcus, Jacob has brainwashed you." she said looking into his eyes.

"Uncle Jacob?" Marcus frowned...

"Yes, brother Jacob helped the dragons to invade our kingdom to attack and he is the spy soldier of King Draco." Arthur told Marcus.

"How can you even say that?" Marcus scrowls.

"Did you remember the day when Henry came to our palace and left the palace without having lunch."

"How can I forget that terrible day? I clearly remember mom! That day you cried all day ...how can I forget that devil man?" Marcus exclaimed gritted his teeth,

"That day Henry came to save us and he gave us all the proof about Jacob betrayal and handed me a golden box that can save us. Henry was afraid that King Draco would definitely attack the Crystal Kingdom to reach the Kingdom snake. Draco is a coward who always backstabbed everyone who trusted him, his devilish greed to rule the magic made him insanely selfish Wizard."

"He knows that he cannot attack the snake as both the kingdoms share the same ancestors. He deliberately attacks the crystal kingdom which made Henry escape by abandoning his beautiful crystal palace."

"You know Marcus he was always worried about us more than his own family. We owed this life to him."

Arthur and Marcus carefully listening to Vincent.

"That day when Henry left a golden box to me and said the box will save us and also the four crystals of the world."

"Four crystals?" Marcus asked furiously interrupting her,

"Yes, four Crystals, You and Arthur are the two of them."

"What mom? We are snakes, aren't we?" Marcus and Arthur widened their eyes in shock.

"You are snakes, son, before that you are the two precious crystals." Vincent continued.

"When I was expecting you, one day I went to visit Henry with your dad. That day the Diamond crystal was at its full power. Diamond crystal was looking for her Heiress. Only a female can be a crystal heiress. Henry has no sister and his parents died leaving him without any other siblings. He was neither married nor had any girlfriend in his life at that time."

"He deliberately introduced me as his sister to the diamond crystal and the diamond crystal also without hesitation accepted me as her heiress and blessed me with two crystals." her eyes glowered with the flash of happy memories.

"We were all very happy the day you both were born, Richard and Henry always wanted you both to grow as snakes and live with the inherited crystal powers, so that whenever in the future if needed you both can save the magical world and.... my sons the time has come."

CHAPTER-27 "UNVEILING THE SECRET"

"We all have to fight the dragons together to win over the Evil Draco..."Vincent said in a roaring voice.

"Mom, I saw Cox jumped in the Valley with dad, he killed our dad mom, how can you say we owe him?" Marcus anxiously asked.

That day when Henry left the golden box with me. The night after that was the full moon night and there was a hidden note written with the magical pen that can only be read under the water.

Your dad riddled me to find the message, "under the yellow moonlight in the blue ambience with a golden companion" I still remember his words.

I solved that riddle and went to my favourite place that is the blue stream, yellow moonlight falling on the blue stream. I dived down the stream with the golden box and opened it, the immense white light glowered on the surroundings and my eye was startled to see the magic crystal...without wasting a moment I opened the note and started reading.

The message written on the note was shocking to me, a tremendous shock wave ran down my body reading it, I couldn't understand what to do..., her eyes filled with emotions reminded the past...

"What was the message, mom?" Arthur asked interestingly...

The message was... "King Dragon backstabbed us, I am losing my kingdom if possible then kindly save my crystals, your helpless brother Henry."

"I read it, again and again, to understand what he meant to save his crystals, then I reminded of his daughters though I wasn't sure of that."

"Yes, I have my two crystals with me that are my sons and Henry mentioned earlier that Dragons are behind the four crystals I have two and the other two crystals are with him, but who were the other two crystals, I couldn't conclude that time,

"I flew to the kingdom of crystal and the disastrous scene made me shiver in shock, corpses of the people of kingdom scattered all over,

Great buildings had turned into rubble, I looked all over for Henry or any other member of the royal family, I couldn't find anyone, I screamed their names..."Lily..."... "Henry..." I ran in the crystal palace, The beautiful glass place had scattered like hell, I couldn't explain how much heart wrenched with the thought of losing them all, losing my only family other than you, I cried insanely, I searched all over in a hope to find someone I kept screaming out their names, My feet were injured by the scattered glasses but couldn't feel the pain that moment as the physical pain is far less than what pain my heart is feeling."

"I searched over and over again at every corner every small place,"

"I was shattered with a thought I took a long time to reach here, I lost them, I was crying then suddenly I saw a small hand buried under the debris of a wooden closet, the fingers were moving,"

"I hurriedly shoved the wooden log, it was very heavy I don't know how I got all that strength and I shove the heavy log aside,"

"I was shocked to see the little princess brutally injured lying half dead, I grabbed her out of the log, and I thanked God she was alive, she was Henry's Princesses...Olivia." tears rolled down her eyes.

"Olivia"... both the princes raised their eyebrows, with their eyes wide open looked at each other in shock.

"Marcus, do you remember when you were about 6 years old, Lily visited us with her infant princess for a short time, that day Arthur and Richard were out of the kingdom. Your eyes glowered to see a small baby, you insisted to hold the baby, though I was afraid that you are so small to hold her, still Lily helped you to hold the little doll in your arms, You looked at her small face and smirkingly you looked at me, with an innocent look, you chuckled..."Mom, she is so beautiful, I am in love with her, I want to marry her when we grow up,... I and Lily were amused to hear that from you, but Lily promised a grand wedding to you with Olivia."

"Do you remember?" Vincent asked knitting her brows looking at Marcus sad face.

Marcus slightly nod shrugging his shoulders and was feeling very sad, thinking of how he behaved with Olivia, he is guilty of what he did to her, he assaulted her, humiliated her many times...he couldn't have the courage to face his mom, he lowered his head and a tear fall on his fist...Arthur noticed his sad face and pressed Marcus shoulder to console him.

"What happened, next mom?" Arthur asked to divert Vincent's gaze from Marcus.

"I took her in my arms and was about to leave the place as it was not safe to stay there for a long time, I was about to move forward then someone attacks me from behind, I couldn't saw his face I turned and enchant a spell on him and he disappeared, I was losing my powers, dizzily,

I enchant another spell and landed in the city of muggles. I knew one muggle who learnt all the wizardry skills and serving the magical world living among the muggles, I went to his place, It was an orphanage. He takes care of the wizard orphans there and helped them raise, learn magic and also educate them as muggles."

"It was a stormy night, I knocked at the door, I was losing my strengths, I difficultly managed to reach him and asked for help to save Olivia, He couldn't recognize me because I was badly injured and my clothes, my looks were all messy, I also didn't disclose my identity as that time we were surrounded by enemies all over and we can't trust anyone.

The man was very humble and kind, he gave us a room to stay and gave all the required first aid to Olivia. By that time, I was assured that he will take good care of Olivia.

I was so tired, I couldn't hold my breath and picture of you three came into my eyes, I collected all my strength and flew back to the palace.

I landed near the valley in the woods, for my shock dragons has already invaded in the kingdom and was attacking us, I hurriedly ran in the palace to find you and Richard.

First, I ran to your room, I heave a sigh of relief to see you both safely playing in your room unaware of the outside attack, I locked your room's door from outside so that you won't come out. I ran to find Richard,

I ran all over the place to find Richard, I saw Jacob talking to some stranger beside the main gate of the Palace, I was about to call his name then suddenly the stranger saw me and raised his wands to me to attack me, I defend my self-hiding behind the wall.

It was Draco, King of Dragons, I enchanted a spell on him and he couldn't defend him wisely and fall on the ground, I ran outside to find Richard, I saw dragons army taking over the Snakes army, I saw Richard, who was courageously fighting and killing down the dragons, Meanwhile a dragon soldier saw me and attacked me, I throw a spell and he died, but injured my right arm, I ran to Richard killing all the dragons coming my way like a warrior, Richard smiled and encouraged me to fight, his last words were, "Together we can defeat dragons forever"...we and our army fought for hours, Draco is such a coward that he cannot dare to fight us face to face, He always used cheat tricks he disguises as Henry approached Richard, I saw them and as I only know that Henry might have died or injured he can't be him, Richard was about to walk towards Henry to help when Richard was just a meter away from Him, Draco turned to his real look and enchant the forbidden killing spell on Richard a flash of light approaching Richard, I ran towards Richard and pushed him hard away from the flash, I enchant a spell and my body turned in a crystal mirror and flash strikes me and flashed back to Draco, before he could understand what happened his spell backfired on him, he dashed to the ground.

I turned to my real look again and faintly fall on the ground,"

"Richard tried telepathy with Henry, his efforts worked with my blurred vision I saw Henry, I couldn't believe my eyes "was it Henry? I kept murmuring to myself, I tried crawling to them as I have no strength to walk on my legs, I was numb because of the forbidden spell before Richard or Henry could find me or I could reach them I saw Draco limping towards them and was about to attack them back, Henry grabbed Richard and jumped into the valley."

"Draco also disappeared with a flash of light."

CHAPTER-28 "JACOB"

"Mom, How about dad and Henry? What happened to them?" Arthur asked... Vincent was lost in the trance of the past

"Yes, mom, the leftover warriors searched them down the valley in the woods for a week but we couldn't find any trace of either of them. Where had they gone? Did they die? "Its a mystery so far for all of us and after waiting for 10 years uncle Jacob regretfully announced him dead," Marcus added.

"How could Jacob even think that?" Vincent frowned.

Arthur heard footsteps outside the room, "Shhh!" He signalled to Vincent to stop saying... Everyone turned to the door,

The door opened and a tall old man entered the room.

"Oh my god, Queen, I am so happy to see you back," Jacob excitedly yelled, the next moment he started pretending to be happy with crocodile tears in his eyes.

He took long treads towards the queens' bed and kneeled shedding more tears...

"Hail Queen Vincent! Welcome back Queen,"... "Queen if possible please forgive me, forgive me because I couldn't save the king that, I was hypnotized by Draco, I am always loyal to the kingdom of snakes and the king, please forgive me."

"If you don't believe ask the princes, I protected them all the time, I raised them as my own kids. I didn't produce my own family. I gave my whole life to the kingdom and the princes. I kept praying for your well being. Queen, I can't explain my happiness to see you awake." He sobs harder covering his face in his hands.

Vincent saw his crocodile tears and hypocritic happiness and apology.

"Jacob, I am also happy to see you after so long, You have raised my kids very well. I appreciate that and also am very thankful to you for taking care of my kids for so long. God heard your prayers and see I am back ...you must visit the church to thank God as soon as possible." Vincent said smirking.

"Yes, Queen as you say. I should thank God for sending you back. I should go to the church, hail the queen." he bowed and hurriedly left the room.

As he left, Vincent rolled her eyes towards both the princes,

"Dear if you both want to get the proof of his betrayal then secretively follow him."

Arthur and Marcus looked at each and without thinking for a while they both enchant a spell and become invisible as now they have the Red moon power, they can change any of the shapes and nobody's power can detect their presence around them. Jacob was hurriedly walking down the aisle with sweat on his forehead as if he is in some urgency.

He went out of the palace and ran towards the lake looking back forth again and again. He reaches the shore of the lake hurriedly took a motorboat and pace up in the lake.

Marcus was shocked to see him going away, "Arthur this is not the way to church." he said being invisible.

"Yes, bro, let us follow him, they now transform into two swans and flew and sat on the edge of Jacob's boat. The boat paced up to the other shore of the lake. He stopped the boat and jumped out the boat, ties the boat top to rock and ran inside the dark cave looking back and forth, he enchants a spell on a piece of rock and the rock turned into a dragon mouth wide open, Arthur and Marcus were astonished to see a dragon shape doorway.

They kept following Jacob.

Jacob hurriedly ran in the dragon door...

Arthur and Marcus hurriedly jumped into the door before it gets closed.

Jacob pace up in a dark way. He was fiercely walking in as he was familiar with this way...

After a moment he took a turn to his right and disappeared.

Arthur and Marcus were shocked by his sudden disappearance.

Arthur checked the walls but there was no hidden door. "What the hell where that damn Jacob disappear?" He groaned.

Marcus was trying to eavesdrop through the wall..."Shh...shh...Put your ears on the wall."

He instructed Arthur.

"Why can't we use our powers?" Arthur asked whispering.

"We can't use powers here Arthur, they will catch us... Shhh... listen to them carefully."

They heard Jacob's voice...

"Vincent was awake now, I doubt whether she disclosed the truth to the princes or not. I kept brainwashing both the boys and I am sure they never trust their mother over me." Jacob said in a submissive tone.

Arthur and Marcus was shocked to hear his words...

Arthur couldn't control his excitement and tried to walk through the wall. He successfully walked through the wall, looking forward to Arthur. Marcus also followed him and trail to the other side of the wall,

Marcus and Arthur landed in a huge room of a palace.

They were shocked to see Jacob was kneeling down in front of a tall figure hidden behind a cloak.

"Who could be that person?" both the boys thinking in their minds.

A loud devilish laugh echoed in the room, with Jacob's confession.

The person in the cloak turned around shoving his cloak, roaring.

"I am DRACO JUNIOR you better be clear with your words you fool." growled at Jacob... Jacob started shivering with his words.

Marcus and Arthur got freezed with their mouth and eyes wide open in shock.

CHAPTER-29 "LUCIFER"

The tall figure that Arthur and Marcus was shocked to see is Prince of Shark, "Lucifer Junior Draco."

"What the hell he is doing here?" Marcus whispered.

"Jacob, you better be more careful now onwards. I am damn sure by the time the three crystals have already been activated by Vincent and before she could find the fourth crystal we should win over them.

Then, nobody can stop me to be the ultimate powerful Emperor of the magic world." Lucifer growled devilishly."

"Yes, Master...Amidst all the danger, I will always be loyal to you." Jacob bowed and walked back through the wall.

Lucifer also went out of the room.

Marcus signalled Arthur to follow Jacob back.

This time they directly teleported themselves back to Vincent's room as they already know Jacob's truth.

"Mom," Vincent was standing near the window lost in her trance and snapped with Arthur's voice.

Both Arthur and Marcus treads towards her and narrated her the whole scene.

"The betrayer exclaimed to be loyal to dragons mom." Marcus chuckled.

"Now, you both understand whom to trust and whom to not," she said looking at both.

"Listen to me careful sons, promise me you will pretend to be normal in front of Jacob. You both continue treating him the same way you did so far ok." Vincent instructed them.

"We promise mom!" three of them shake hands and promised Vincent.

Arthur thought to tell Vincent about Olivia but was not sure how to introduce her... an idea stricks his mind and he asked to leave.

"Mom, I have some urgent thing to do so, I have to go. If you want me you can mind link with me anytime." he just ran out of the room,

Marcus stays with Vincent as he wants to spend some good time with his mom...

"I want to share the darkest secret of my life with you, mom," Marcus said fidgeting with his fingers.

"Mom, I am sorry I never wanted to do that but what mindset we had about uncle Henry and his family maddens me."

He gasps...

"I grew up all the way to take revenge with King Cox, in the quench of revenge... I..I... did that..." he burst into tears his voice getting deeper.

"What are you saying, Marcus?" Vincent squat in front of Marcus and tightly hold his hand.

"Mom..., I Kidnapped Olivia..., I assaulted her...I am ashamed of what I did. The demon overcomes me but mom believe me I am guilty...guilty of my sins and ready to get punished." he starts sobbing.

"Mom, She is my first love and I just ruined her dignity she kept pleading for mercy, but I was so blind to have my revenge that I couldn't trust her innocence... I am sorry mom."

"I tried to cover up ... I even apologised to her many times but she didn't forgive me. she ran away from me...she hates me mom, My love of the life hates me... I destroyed my relationship before it starts." he gasps.

"I want her mom, I want to marry her the way I wished when I held her for the first time. I won't survive without her."

"Yes, Mom, I am in love with her again...I will be nothing without her...please mom please forgive me, I know you are ashamed of me right now. Maybe you are feeling like hitting me...please hit me, do whatever you want to punish me, just bring her back to me...just bring her back mom," he said slapping his face.

"Stop it! Marcus, stop it! You did nothing," she hugged him.

Marcus sobs harder shrugging in Vincent's arm.

"Marcus..., it's true that you kidnapped Olivia to take the revenge but baby. It was our plan for you to catch her before dragons could reach her." She said unfolding another secret.

"What???... What did you just say, mom?" Marcus perplexedly asked.

Vincent gap like a fish.

"Well, I don't know where to start from?" she sighs...

"Emmm...em... I think I should start since the day of the attack."

"I slipped into the state of coma after the attack, though my mind was awake I can see you all. I can hear everything around me. I saw how Jacob brainwashed you both with his lies about Henry."

'After a week, I got a mind link signals from your dad."

"DAD???" Marcus jumped off his chair.

"Calm down Marcus!"

"Yes, your dad, he is alive and safe with Henry...or I can say Henry saved him that day."

"That is how we owe him our lives, son." she huffed.

"Mom, is DAD alive...??? How... When...?" Where is he??" He curiously asked going back forth in the room.

CHAPTER-30 "FIGHTING FOR THE GIRL"

"Mom, please come up." he groans.

"Yes!...yes!...Richard is alive!" She screamed ...

"Do you know..., Marcus Who saved your dad?" she chuckled turning to Marcus.

Marcus shrugs his shoulders in anticipation.

"Henry..." he guessed.

"Yes, Marcus, you got it right...Henry... my brother, Richard's best friend saved him from death," she smirks looking at Marcus confused looks.

"But mom, Jacob told me that Henry pushed dad down to death, and saved himself." he scoffed.

"That is what he was here with you for so long son." Vincent frowned.

"Jacob stayed here to mind wash the only survivors of The kingdom of snakes, that is you and Arthur, he did it purposely Marcus, Jacob is a puppet in hands of Draco," she added

"Holy shit... and me being a fool as always keep trusting his fake stories, his fake concerns about the kingdoms and blindly kept tailing him since you guys left... what a fool I am? I should have cross-checked when I grew up in all my senses, besides that I started burning the flames of revenge...How could I forget our familiar relationship with King Cox, his love to me....How could I forget all those happy moments we spent together? How could I?" Marcus scowls himself pulling his hair in shame and frustration.

"We don't have time for your regrets Marcus, Maybe later, you can apologise for all your deads," Vincent said.

"All right mom," Marcus said wiping his face with his hands. Vincent continued...

"Henry jumped down the valley with Richard as you know the valley down there is a secret door to many kingdoms and one of them is 'The kingdom of the sea'."

"Henry has a friendly relationship with the whales and mermaids wizards. They help Henry and Richard to hide there safely from as long as they want to."

"Draco can never dare to invade in the kingdom of the sea as the wizard emperor is his father-in-law, after the demise of Draco's wife neither Draco visited them nor anyone from the sea contacted him. It's well said, we should always count on enemies rather than friends. He always underestimates the power of the kingdom of the sea and never bothers to win over them. But, the emperor of the kingdom of the sea 'Zohan Mason' has deep grudges on him because Draco inherited his evil mindset to his grandson."

"Zohan many times tried to educate Lucifer the goodwill and tries hard to inherit the righteous but all his efforts went in vain. Zohan thought to hand over the responsibility of a region of his kingdom and later Crowned Lucifer the Prince of the Sharks. Lucifer became more powerful and as his veins have the evil blood running all over his body, he showed his true colours there as well."

"He came to be the evil prince ever a kingdom can have. That is why Emperor Zohan always kept it secret that he saved Henry and Richard. Zohan is enemy with Draco, but Draco always used Lucifer as a shield. Zohan is helpless when it comes to Lucifer as he is the only grandson he has. Now, Zohan has made his mindset clear about Lucifer as well. He now wants the well-being of the magical world at any cost. Lucifer and Draco are still unaware of his plans." She explained and looks around before continuing.

Marcus looks around too... "Don't worry mom, Nobody can eavesdrop or sneak in this room. It is a secret enchanted room." He said.

"I know that son. Still, we should never underestimate our enemies. Zohan took proper care of Richard and Henry both are healthy and safe in the kingdom of sea, Now I need to execute what they have planned so far to win over Dragons." she said writhing in anger.

"Yeah, tell me, mom," Marcus said straightening up his back.

"Let us go to Arthur first," Vincent said.

"Ok mom, I just check where he is?" Marcus pulls out his mobile to call Arthur.

Arthur after leaving the room went straight to Olivia's room but he didn't find her there and then he ran to the garden to search for her.

He saw Olivia alone sitting under the tree lost in her trance He excitedly walked to her and sits beside her.

"Hey Olivia, Missing me?" he chortled and Olivia snaps out of his trance.

"Oh, Arthur, you scared me." she winks turning to him.

"Yeah, I missed you so much." she chuckled glancing at him.

"Oh as in that's great! I mean, not great, but just that," he breaks off, looking nervous.

"Ok Olivia, I want to ask you something." He takes a deep breath, his pupils dilated so his irises were just a thin strip of blue circling his pupils...

Olivia continuously stares at him and listens to him carefully..." Olivia will you ...will you mm..." he clusters..."I have some feelings for you maybe a feeling of love."

"How dare you say that Arthur...??" Marcus groaned cutting off Arthur.

CHAPTER-31 "FAMILY DINNER"

"How dare you, Arthur? How could you even say or even feel like that for her?" Marcus frowned walking to them with Vincent.

Arthur and Olivia jerked with Marcus harsh words and stands up from their places and looked at them coming.

"What bro? You already tried your luck and she refused you."

"Shut up, Arthur," Marcus growled moving forward and raising his hand on Arthur.

"Stop it, Marcus," Vincent screamed from behind and Marcus freezed for a moment and took his hand away.

She hurriedly moved to them.

"This is not the way you brothers should ever talk to each other and nor the right place." She snaps his fingers and all the four disappears and landed in Vincent's room.

"Mom, you know I have a feeling for Olivia, how could I let Arthur propose to her?" Marcus yelled pointing his finger to Arthur looking at Olivia.

"But mom...," Vincent raises her hand to Arthur to shut his mouth.

"Is this the right time for you to fight for a girl... I never thought my boys to be so stupid and selfish?"

"We are going through such a critical situation, a sword of death is swinging on all of us and you are fighting with each other for a girl...Oh Jeez!" She frowned throwing her hands in the air.

"I am sorry mom!" Arthur kneeled in front of Vincent and embarrassedly apologised for his kiddish behaviour.

So, does Marcus apologised.

"It's ok, I don't want any mess in between you both, firstly, let me clear one thing. So, that you don't mess up again with each other."

She turned and moved to Olivia who is silently standing glancing at everyone.

"Let me introduce you to the fourth magical crystal," Vincent announced giving a side hug to Olivia.

"She is Henry's daughter and the princess of the crystal kingdom... "ZENIA COX"

"What...???" Arthur and Marcus raised their brows, shockingly screamed in unison.

 Vincent snaps his finger a girl's in a white cloak appeared in front of everyone.

Arthur and Marcus astonishingly looking at her..."Who is she mom?" Marcus freaked out.

She slowly shoved her cloak disclosing her identity.

Arthur and Marcus freaked out and shockingly step back, a knot went down their throats with their eyes wide open, pendulums their eyes from ZENIA to the other girl.

Arthur rubbed his eyes, rolled his eyes again and gap like fish twice... but nothing came out of his mouth.

Marcus winks for a while and turned his sight to Vincent who is continuously smirking looking at her traumatized sons.

Marcus runs his hands in his hair and moved to Vincent.

"This is not fair mom...You are taking long to introduce the new guest here." Marcus huffs looking at the girls.

"She is...Olivia...Olivia Cox."

Marcus gulps and gap like a fish...Froze for a moment hearing it.

"What???" He screamed in shock...

"Woah Woah. "Arthur snapped...

 "Mom don't tell me, we going to have an identical princess as our life partners," Arthur asked.

"I am more than happy to stamp on your words Arthur, you are right my son!" Vincent exclaimed smirking taking Olivia towards Marcus.

She grabbed Olivia's hand and handed Olivia hands in Marcus's hand. "She is your princess and will remain yours forever." She exclaimed bonding their hands together.

Marcus' eyes sparkled looking at Olivia and Olivia shyly looking at him stealing glances blushing...

Arthur got excited with a butterfly dancing in his stomach when Vincent grabs Zenia's hand and handed her to Arthur..." She is your princess my son...your love..." she chortled...

Arthur blushed hearing that and hugged Vincent..." I love you mom," with wet eyes he kisses his mom on her cheeks...Emotions welled up in Vincent's eyes too..you better show love to Zenia... Zenia blushed shyly winking at Arthur.

"This is so freaking unbelievable mom," "Will you please explain?" Marcus sneered laughing running his hand in his hair and another hand on his waist.

"Long story Marcus, I need to take a break...I am hungry." Vincent huffed folding her hand close to her chest.

"How about a reunion dinner Mom?"... Arthur chuckled

"Wow!, let's go...I am so happy to have a family dinner after ages, I wish dad to be here." Arthur said smiling looking at all...

"I regret to say this Arthur, but we can't show all of our cards, not at this stage, not now." Vincent sadly stated.

"Why mom?"... Arthur frowned...

"Arthur, Don't you remember, we have a spy here. Jacob..."Vincent scowls.

"Oh! yes, Sorry I was so overwhelmed, I forgot everything around." Arthur chuckled.

"We all are overwhelmed, I am happy to get things on the right track after decades," Vincent said happily looking at all.

"Zenia will be visible to us all but will remain invisible to everyone other than us."

"So, don't worry, Arthur...you have enough quality time to spend with her." Vincent chortled...

Everyone laughed and giggles echoed in the room...

"Thank you, mom," Arthur hugged Vincent and Marcus joined them..."I too thank you, mom."

"Ok, let's celebrate our reunion...Marcus chuckled...Olivia went back to her room with invisible Zenia.

Arthur, Vincent and Marcus moved to the dining room.

Vincent was amazed to see her palace again after ages..." Nothing has changed" she said with tears fledging in her eyes.

Arthur hold her hand and helped her move down the stairs.

"You guys maintained my home so well...I am proud of you kids."

"We are a grown-up mom." Marcus giggled...

"Yeah! grown-up adults, who were fighting an hour ago over a girl as they fight for toys at the age of 10."

Vincent chortled again and three of them laugh...

"Let's have dinner mom...today we will be going to have all of your favourite dishes," Marcus said grabbing a chair for Vincent...

A man in his late 40s bowed to Vincent,

"Mom, he is Bob, our chief chef and she is Charity Olivia's caretaker." Marcus introduces the staff to Vincent.

"Oh, wow nice to meet you all," Vincent said smiling.

"Let us start," she said taking a spoon.

Elsa the Buttler started serving them.

"Ohh, uncle Jacob is also here," Arthur smirked looking at Jacob who was coming to them...

Vincent turned to Jacob, "Jacob come let's have dinner." she said gesturing Jacob to the vacant chair opposite to hers.

"How could I share the same place with the queen?" Jacob submissively said bowing to Vincent.

"Oh! come on, Jacob, you raised my kids so well, you are also a family to us...come don't hesitate."

She smiles and again gestures him to the vacant chair.

"Ok, Queen, if you insist." he took a chair...everyone started enjoying the dinner.

CHAPTER-32 "LOVE IS IN THE AIR"

All of them have casual talks at the dinner table, after finishing the dinner peacefully. Arthur and Marcus took Vincent to her room, help her to lay on the bed. She soon fell asleep.

Arthur and Marcus couldn't control their emotions anymore and ran to Olivia's room while crossing his room.

"Wait, Arthur." Marcus asked Arthur to wait and went to his room to fetch a bottle of wine. "we should celebrate with our girls too," Marcus said with a wide smile holding the wine bottle, "wow that's Great bro, Arthur responded with an ear to ear smile.

They moved to Olivia's room, as they knock on the door both were looking very nervous,

Marcus was confused and nervous about how to restart with Olivia and Arthur was looking for a way, how to start with Zenia.

Olivia opens the door and shyly smile looking at Marcus. Zenia was there in the room in the invisible state though she was visible to them sitting on the sofa.

"Hi, girls…can we come in?" Arthur courteously asked.

"Certainly yes…" Oliva answered,

They entered the room, Marcus enchants the room with a spell so that no one can hear them.

Zenia and Olivia are identical twins and very similar to each other,

It's very difficult for the boys to decide to sit with whom as Zenia is visible to them as well so they couldn't discriminate between the two princesses.

Hesitate to sit, they both looked at each others faces.

"Take your seat boys," Zenia said smirking looking at the confused boys.

"Eh... hmm..." Marcus cleared his throat and a knot went down his throat, "Actually..." he paused and looked at Arthur who's just rotating his eyeballs like a pendulum from one girl to another girl.

"I never thought the demon I met the first day will be so shy meeting his would-be wife like this..." Olivia chuckled smirking looking at Marcus.

Marcus' eyes lit up with her words and he confidently moved to Olivia.

"I am really sorry and embarrassed too for what I did. You can punish the way you want" Marcus whisper leaning to Olivia for a hug.

Arthur hurriedly jumped beside Zenia.

"Dr Arthur seems very excited about his girl. Zenia shyly Giggled..." Arthur's cheeks turn pink blushing and stealing a glance at Zenia.

"Let us start it in a new way." Marcus screams waving his hands in the air." Yes, the brother said it right." we should refresh our start.

Marcus kneels in front of Olivia, grab her hand and bow.

"I Prince Marcus Smith with all my heart apologise to Princess Olivia Cox.

"Would you like to start a new journey with me?" Marcus asked looking into her eyes in hope.

Olivia covered her face with her other hand and a tear of happiness rolled down her cheeks, Zenia who is sitting next to her gave her a side hug. "Go on sis". She whispered in her ears...

"Yes, I love to," Olivia chuckled and kissed his head.

Marcus kisses her hand and sits next to her even closer to her than before and kissed her shoulder..." I apologise once again." He whispered in her ear, Olivia blushed and patted his hand winking at him.

Zenia looked at Arthur squeezing her eyes as if she is expecting the same from Arthur.

Arthur understood her gestures and shrug his shoulder in anticipation.

"What?" she whispered.

"It will be a special moment in a special way," My special girl deserves the best". Arthur chuckled and give her a peck on the cheek, she blushed touching her kissed cheek and her face turned red.

Marcus brings four glasses and poured the wine and handed everyone a glass of wine.

This one is for our friendship, he screams raising a toast, cheers.

"Cheers," the atmosphere lightened up with warmth, they laughed, enjoyed the couple's dance and couple moments,

"Arthur, hope you mind spending some alone time with Zenia," suddenly Marcus chuckled and asked Arthur to leave with Zenia.

Arthur excitedly nodded and left them alone.

"You shouldn't do that Master," Olivia chortled standing with the arms crossed to her chest.

"Don't embarrass me Oliv...you can call me by my name," Marcus responded kissing her forehead...

Arthur and Zenia appeared in front of Arthur's room, Arthur covered Zenia eyes before entering the room,

"What are doing, Arthur?" Zenia curiously asked.

"Have patience darling." he opens the door.

Arthur removes his hand from her eyes, she opens her eyes and her eyes sparkled with the view around the room, the light is off, the scented candles light the room faintly, the room is beautifully decorated with roses, the overall ambience is so romantic!, She turned to him and surprised to see Arthur kneeling down, "Oh My God!" she covers her mouth in astonishment looking at him in surprise!

"I Prince Arthur Smith commits my whole life to Princess Zenia Cox. Arthur proposed her raising a beautiful heart-shaped diamond ring..."Will you accept me?" Arthur asked.

"When did you plan all this?" Zenia counter questioned him looking around.

"Will you accept me, Princess Zenia Cox?"

"Yes, I Do!" ..."This is beautiful!" she said kneeling down in front of Arthur and kissed him on his lips,

Arthur grabs her lips for another kiss and the soft kiss turned to an intense, intimate kiss,

Both parted their lips away panting and breathing heavenly.

"You are gorgeous indeed Zenia," he whispered in her ear kissing her earlobes,

"When did you plan this?" Zenia chuckled pushing him away.

"The moment you squeeze your eyes on me," he said running his hand in his hair,

"I told you it will going to be special." He smirked.

"I am impressed." Zenia giggled.

Arthur took her into his arms in bridal style, she wraps her arms around his neck continuously looking into his deep blue eyes and puts her on the bed,

She slightly blushes when Arthur's face was an inch away from her face while putting her down on the bed.

Arthur lays down next to her by her side, "Hope we can talk if you are not tired or feeling sleepy." he sweetly asked.

Zenia turned by her side facing Arthur, "Yes we can talk!" she affirmed.

"I know Arthur you have so many thoughts and questions in your head," she said brushing his cheeks with her fingers... his face heated up with her touch he slightly slides to her and wraps his arm around her, she rests her head on his shoulder and her hand on his chest.

She started narrating the story.

On the other hand, in Olivia's room.

 Marcus and Olivia were quietly sitting on the bed with their heads resting on the head of the bed,

"Oliv..." Marcus calls her name breaking the silence.

She didn't respond sitting next to him with her eyes closed, Marcus turned towards her, he knew that she is not yet asleep.

"Are you still afraid of me, Oliv?" he mutters looking at her face...she remained silent again.

"I apologise Oliv and I promise I will never harm you ever again, I promise...you can punish me whichever way you like...please Oliv, Please speak up, your silence is killing me, please." he started sobbing in his hands.

Olivia opened her eyes and tightly wrapped her arms around him, "you better stay on your promise, Marcus."

Marcus jerked with her sudden reactions and clenched her in his arms...hugging her tightly...As she looks up, she finds his blue eyes full of apology, passion, love, desire, and questions. Yes, they are looking for answers looking into each others eyes.

CHAPTER-33 ZENIA'S TRUTH

Zenia started the story from the day before Olivia's kidnapping.

"Since your childhood, you both trusted Jacob and he kept pondering hatred about us in your hearts and brains. Queen continuously informed all his deeds to the king via telepathy."

"Though you follow Jacob the mindset behind his every move was of Draco. In the beginning, Jacob convinced Marcus to kidnap the crystal princess on the stake of revenge, so they planned to implant a girl in the place of Olivia. So that they can have one more spy of Dragons in the kingdom Snake which will be closer to Marcus. It must be for some sort of his personal gain. Draco found a new way, he is the biggest betrayer he has his trust issues, not even Jacob. He wanted to conquer the snake Kingdom by implanting his daughter and later he planned a forced marriage of Marcus and his daughter. The girl he wanted to replace was his daughter. 'Diana' but as we already knew his plan. Dad replaced Diana with Olivia once again. Jacob neither knows Olivia nor Diana, so he couldn't discriminate between the one who is present in the Palace and considered Olivia as Draco's daughter."

"So, when he gets to know about the kidnap, he was very happy as he was thinking that Diana enters the palace with your consent. But, it was our plan. Dad wanted Olivia to be in the palace so that she can help the queen to come out of the coma with her crystal wizardry skills because only a crystal heiress can help the crystal to come out of her trouble. But we never thought of Marcus, to behave like this with Olivia 'he badly assaulted her' and that's actually broke her. She, therefore, decided to run away from the Palace and to abort the mission and then she ran out of the Palace to escape. She lived her life in an orphanage because of that, she's quite afraid of things like all the other muggles do. She learnt all the wizardry skills only for the sake of doing it but never thoroughly considered her a wizard, Dad convinced her to be a part of the missions but when she met us after so many years she was overwhelmed with emotions and her strength, her family becomes her weakness."

"When she ran away from the palace and blacked out in the woods king Richard thought of a change in the plan to replace Olivia with me before your men can reach Olivia, she was replaced. Marcus got me instead of Olivia."

"She was sent back to the Kingdom of Whales where dad, Mom and Richard helped her to come out of the trauma and to get her more strength to face the Dragons. They made her understand that this is part of the mission, nothing to worry about as she lost her virginity to his would-be husband. Mom helped her come out of the guilt. It doesn't matter to her. It was very difficult for her to overcome. Though the way Marcus treated her was very unexpected, they tried to make her understand how important the mission is for all of them. It took her a lot of time to understand what exactly we are up to? And till that time, I stay in the Palace with both of you and you get to know me better than Marcus because he was ashamed of what he did to Olivia. He tried apologising to me, but I couldn't forgive him as it was not me the one who he humiliated. So, I thought of waiting. For the day to come for him to apologise to the right person. The day you both went for the Red Moon competition. I helped the Queen to get out of the coma and there you caught her awake, but you were still not aware of me."

"Bingo, I am a Code crystal."

Arthur smirked looking at Zenia, "that is why Marcus's date was disastrous." he chuckled.

"Yes..." she giggled shyly.

"Can I ask something to you Zen?" he asked.

"Hmm..." she permitted.

"Did you ever had feelings for me, since we met?" he asked looking into her eyes.

"I ..em.. honestly...I initially didn't feel anything because there was no place for love in my mission, later I started feeling for you, the way you treated me, the way you love Alice, your kind, humble and soft touches pulled me into you."

"And yes, I fall for you, and I realised I love Arthur." she gave a peck on his lips.

"What...?" Arthur asked widening his eyes.

"Come again, Miss." He whines.

"I LOVE YOU," she shouted jumping off the bed...Arthur jumped to her and pulled her from her waist, pushing his lips on hers.

On the other hand, the same story was narrated by Olivia to Marcus she was still quite afraid of him.

Marcus kept apologising for the whole night.

Olivia couldn't completely forgive him still for the sake of her parents, she gave him a second chance.

CHAPTER-34 "TRAITOR"

The next morning, after having the breakfast all of them gathered in Vincent's room for further planning.

Vincent explained their strategy to them and decided to visit the kingdom of whales tonight.

"All agreed." Arthur and Marcus left for work whereas Olivia stayed with the queen and Zenia have to go back to her parents.

Marcus spends his day working very normally with Jacob.

Jacob informed him about the company's new project in between, he kept asking Marcus about the queen's health and what she talked to him about. Marcus understood his intentions. He smartly makes himself engaged in back-to-back meetings with the clients and delegates from a foreign country. He already instructed Tom and Fin about his next days busy schedule.

These days he was so occupied with his family that he couldn't give much time to his company and business, moreover, the coming days will also be hectic for him emotionally and physically both. Tonight, it will be going to be a rollercoaster of emotions as he is going to meet his father after 15 years, whom everyone considered dead. Even the thought made me overwhelmed.

Jacob didn't find anything suspicious about Marcus behaviour. So, he decided to check on Arthur, after lunch, Jacob leaves the company building saying that he is not feeling well and going back to the palace for some rest.

Marcus understood that Jacob now wants to have an eye on Arthur. As soon as Jacob left the company, Marcus informed Arthur about Jacob coming back to the Palace.

Arthur was also spending his day in his hospital with patients as usual.

As expected, Jacob went straight to Arthur's hospital. Jacob asked every staff member about Arthur's daily routine... He went to Eden. She is Arthur's Personal Assistant and chief medical officer of the hospital. Jacob cunningly started the conversation with Eden asking her to examine him as he is not feeling well.

"Hello, Ms Eden," Jacob greeted entering her cabin.

Eden was sitting on her chair studying a patients surgery report. She was shocked to see Jacob.

She stood up from her chair and bowed to him...

"Hello, Mr Jacob please have a seat... how can I help you?" she courteously asked.

"I am not feeling well today," Jacob said pressing his forehead.

"Do you have a headache?" she asked.

"Actually, I am feeling very low these days, I am always very worried about my kids my princes." Jacob sadly said.

"Let me check your blood pressure." she fetched the machine and put a cap on Jacob's finger and started examining his pulse rate.

"Not to worry sir, your pressure and pulse are normal, you need not worry about Dr. Arthur. Our hospital is doing very well and soon we will be going to have our new branch in the city. Dr. Arthur is a dedicated medical professional, he loves his profession. He has a bright future as a medical practitioner, his medicines are miraculous and I think master Marcus is also grown up as the best businessman in town under your supervision. You raised both the princes well sir. They respect you a lot. Both the boys always considered you and only you as their family." Eden deliberately praises Jacob.

"You are a magician Ms. Eden, I am feeling better now." Jacob felt relieved hearing her words.

"By the way, Ms. Eden, where is Arthur?" he asked getting out of her cabin,

"Doctor has two consecutive surgeries in the evening. He is discussing the details with his team," she answered.

"Oh, how come you are here?" he curiously asked her.

"I came here to collect the latest reports of the same patient, I was about to leave when you entered Mr. Jacob," She confidently answered again.

"Mr. Jacob, why don't you come with me to meet Dr. Arthur?"... she asked.

"No...Em...I think... I shouldn't disturb him in his meeting." Jacob answered.

He immediately went to his room and informed the Dragon Prince about the under control situation in the palace.

He was so relieved and fell asleep.

On the dinner table, everyone was quietly having their food.

Arthur, Marcus and Vincent behaved calm and composed whereas Jacob was looking for some information about what they are planning.

"Queen, I advised you to visit Arthur's hospital and our company. You will be very happy to see how well I raised your kids and how successful they are in their respective fields," Jacob asked pretending,

"I loved your idea, Jacob, surely will visit their workplace someday, You know I am not that healthy enough to move much. Hope you understand." Queen answered sipping her soup.

Jacob nodded and continued eating.

"How about Olivia, Jacob? Don't you think I should meet her too?"...She chuckled.

Marcus was shocked to hear that and dropped his spoon.

"O..oo...Olivia...." a knot went down his throat with his eyes widen...Jacob looked at Marcus,

Marcus winked at him..."Mom knew everything about our revenge uncle and she is with us on that."

Marcus said.

Jacob heaved a deep sigh,

"Certainly, Queen, whenever you feel good you can visit Olivia?... but I advised you to better stay away from her. Marcus has done half of the job, soon the Cox's family surrender themselves to us, then you can take your husband's death revenge from them." Jacob devilishly smirked.

Queen's blood started boiling listening to his words but she pretends to be calm so does Arthur and Marcus.

"Uncle, I think mom should stay away from that, we both are enough for that girl," she will pay every day and every night for his father's sins, Arthur said grunting his teeth.

"NO! NO! Arthur, I think you should also stay away, Marcus is enough for her." Jacob frowned.

Marcus grin looking at the Queen and Arthur.

"Why so uncle we are mutually on this. So, Arthur should also help me in that." Marcus chuckled...

"Why don't you understand Marcus, she couldn't bear that assault we should have some pity on her," Jacob muttered.

"Pitty...what pitty? She is here to pay for her father's sin, and she will pay according to us." Marcus screamed punching the table and his plate fell and scattered.

Jacob frightened...

"I agree, son but try and understand your father disciples never allow you to do that." Jacob was frightened and tried to calm Marcus down.

"I don't know anything...she has to be punished" Marcus yelled and angrily walked towards Olivia's room.

Jacob moved to the Queen...before he could say anything.

"I don't know what you guys have planned. Kindly let me stay away from this. I trust Marcus and Arthur whatever they will do, I agree with that."Queen sneered and left for her room Arthur helped her go back to her room.

CHAPTER-35 "REUNION"

Marcus moved towards Olivia's room and entered her room without knocking.

"Oops Sorry," he jittered closing his eyes and going out of her room closing the door.

"You can come in, Marcus," Olivia said zipping her dress.

Marcus entered the room lowering his gaze to the floor,

"I am sorry, I should have knocked on the door," he said embarrassedly.

"It's okay, you need not be formal with me." she shyly replied.

"Hmm."

"When are we leaving?" Olivia curiously asked.

"Soon, I am just here to have a check on you," he said stepping forward to her.

"Don't worry I won't run away now." she chuckled.

"I won't even let you." Marcus smoldered clenching her close to him.

His warm minty breath fans her cheeks and she turned pink, blushed looking into his eyes.

/

"Don't ever leave me again Oliv, you mean a lot to me, I want to make love to you, the love you deserve and most important I haven't got my forgiveness yet."

"I will keep trying until you didn't feel like forgiving my sins," Marcus said holding her hand, his blue eyes boring into her browns.

"Sorry to disturb you love birds,"...Vincent chortled coming into their room with Arthur tailing her...

Marcus and Olivia snap hearing her words.

"Mom...I... we..." Marcus stammer.

"It's time to leave Marcus, "Arthur said cutting him off.

"How about Jacob?"... Marcus furiously asked

"Jacob is in deep sleep .... ENCHANTED DEEP SLEEP" Arthur emphasized sneering,

Everyone slightly giggled.

Vincent raised her hand with her palm up...everyone holds her hand...she enchants a spell and they all disappeared. They all landed near the hot water stream,

Olivia was amused to see the stream, "I always wonder why I was attracted to this stream; Now I got the answer because this is the doorway to my parents, my family, my..." her eyes fledged with tears.

"Everything will be fine Oliv," Marcus said wiping her tears with his hands. Marcus holds her hand and holds it tightly throughout their walk into the stream. Arthur was holding Vincent.

The stream ended in a sea, the underwater empire of the whales.

Vincent gave everyone a pill to chew. "Have this, kids, this pill will help you breathe and walk under the water."

"Be careful guys, the danger is everywhere even here as well," Vincent instructed.

Arthur and Marcus were amazed to see a huge palace, a water palace indeed.

Olivia has been to this place earlier she is quite familiar with the atmosphere.

Water is clean and clear with all underwater natural greenery, marine life swimming everywhere around them.

Algae floating around beautiful mermaids some with colourful tails, some have golden tails.

"Amazing!" Arthur muttered.

Whales and sharks guarded the water Palace, letting them into the palace.

"Are they all wizards mom...?" Arthur curiously asked,

"Yes son, they all are royal wizard guards. They guard the kingdom of Sea. You will be amazed to know that the Kingdom of the sea is the wealthiest Wizard kingdom of the magical world."

"Mom, have you been here earlier?" Marcus questioned again.

"I and Princess of the sea were best friends, I used to visit her on vacations and attended her wedding with the cruel Draco," Vincent said pacing in the palace...

"Easy mom, where are you going?" Arthur yelled running behind her...Marcus and Olivia followed them.

"She sensed her love." Olivia whines.

"What...? You mean Dad...?" Marcus screamed.

Olivia winks and nods.

"Mom, wait ..." Marcus yelled pacing forth to Vincent.

Suddenly Zenia appeared in front of them, stopping them to move further.

"What happened?" Vincent groaned.

Zenia bowed to the queen.

"Queen, I need to inform you of something very important before you enter,"

"Firstly, you need to control your feeling in front of the king, and secondly don't make him much overwhelmed."

"The attack weakened his heart and a sudden hike in emotion can be hazardous to him." she politely warned them.

"Heart ...?" Vincent muttered.

"I want to see him let me go in, Zenia." Queen frowned.

Arthur and Marcus came forward and holded Vincent from either side.

"We will take care of that, thank you for informing us, Zenia," Arthur said with a happy face

Three of them entered the room, Zenia and Olivia followed them.

Everything is made up of water here though non-transparent as similar as a normal cemented house we have on land.

Vincent slightly pushes the door to open.

An old man in royal attire standing in front of them.

"Richard..." Vincent whines running to him.

She tightly wrapped her arms around him.

"Ohh, Richard, I'm so glad to see you...I missed you so much." tears kept rolling down her cheeks.

"I missed you my love," Richard said kissing her,

"Dad!" Marcus and Arthur whispered in unison holding back their tears.

Vincent snaped and slightly parted.

Richard, can you recognize them, Vincent asked raising her hands towards the boys.

"My boys...My ultimate winners," Richard screamed stretching his arms for them to hug him overwhelming with emotions.

"Dad...Dad," Both the princes hurriedly moved to him and tightly hugged him.

"Dad, I am so glad to see you, "Arthur said wiping Richards's cheeks.

Everyone with wet eyes and smiling faces looking at each other. The happy family picture is complete now.

"Where are Henry and Lily?" Vincent asked rolling her eyes around.

CHAPTER-36 "EVIL"

Henry and Lily appeared in the room hand in hand.

Vincent moved towards them drenched in tears.

"Ohh, brother...I am so glad to see you," Vincent emotionally said hugging Henry.

"I am glad to see you too Sis"...Henry responded caressing her hair.

"You fulfilled your promise brother, you protected my world, my family, you gave me back my happiness, I owe you everything." Vincent was overwhelmed with happiness.

"Sisters never owe anything to their brothers Vincent other than love." Lily chuckled rubbing Vincent's arm.

"Lily...I missed you so much." Vincent sobbed harder on Lily's shoulder.

The room immediately filled with emotions everyone trailing down memory lane.

Giggles, tears, joy....lots of emotions in everyone's word.

"No more emotions guys," Arthur yelled jumping off his chair.

"I think it's time to serve the purpose we are here..." he seriously said.

"Yes, we are saved because of a purpose, and we should concentrate on that," Richard said joining Arthur.

"We have a plan, a strategical plan to fight and defeat dragons," Henry said.

Every eye turned to Henry.

They sit in a circle so that everyone can hear and see the strategical plan of the attack.

"This time we won't wait for dragons to attack us first, we won't give them any chance to overcome us," Lily considerably said.

"So, what's the plan?" Marcus curiously asked raising his brows.

"Next week on Lucifer's 25th birthday Draco will be going to crown his only son as the King of Dragons. Our plan starts from that day itself..." Henry informed everyone.

"What...New King of Dragons?" Arthur and Marcus muttered in unison.

"Yes, New king of Dragons. Draco who suffered the forbidden killing spell got severely injured and lost his legs and wizardry powers in that attack." Henry explained.

Arthur and Marcus gave an astonishing look to each other.

"So...it means Draco is as good as dead...he is a harmless ass"... Arthur chuckled.

"No...no...We should not underestimate him, Arthur." Vincent groaned.

"Sorry...mom," he replied lowering his head.

"Listen to me carefully, I know you four have a lot many questions in your head, I will definitely answer them all one by one, first of all, you need to understand the exact situation," Henry said pointing to the four youngsters...Arthur, Olivia, Zenia and Marcus.

Four of them nodded.

"What I am going to tell you now is more fascinating than your imagination..." Henry continued.

"Draco has a backup of his powers stored in his crown. The person who wears the crown will automatically get his powers." he meticulously enchants the crown with his all powers, long before the attack"

"Now, we have to destroy the crown, not Draco...before it will transfer its power to Lucifer." Henry was very calmly explaining...

"Lucifer is a good man so far... it's only Draco who trying and pushing him into the evils..." Zohan" King of the Kingdom of sea enters the room saying.

Everyone turned to his voice. Vincent stood from her chair and bowed to him.

"He is King Zohan"...Vincent introduced him to her sons.

Arthur and Marcus also bowed to him.

"It is an immense pleasure to have you all here, I am truly stoked to see you all..." Zohan whines...his voice is bold and deep.

"You came in at the right time Zohan, Come join us..." Richard said.

"I am already in, my friend." Zohan giggled...

Everyone laughed at his words.

"Ohk back to the plan guys." Zohan roared taking a seat next to Henry.

"The situation is much more complex than it appears," Zohan exclaimed looking at Arthur and Marcus.

"Yes," Richard added.

"As I told you about the Crown ceremony, the event going to be a grand celebration. Draco will invite the whole magical world, so do you guys." Henry again said pointing to the Snake Princes.

By this time Arthur and Marcus understood that they will be going to play an important role in this planning.

"As you know...so far, he is unaware of our existence, he considered us dead." Richard smirks turning his eyes on Henry and Lily.

They all smirk exchanging their gaze.

"Nonetheless we should not ignore the fact that Draco still has some superpowers with him." Zohan again exclaimed.

"Hmm..." Henry and Richard in unison.

"We have the Red Moon Powers why we are afraid of his so-called superpowers?" Arthur arrogantly Whines.

"Ohh, son..." Zohan heaves a sigh.

"I agree with Marcus, we are superiorly powered in any way. We have the Red moon powers." Arthur exclaimed showing his red wand.

"I regret to say that Draco...has THE BLACK MOON powers saved in his crown." he saddens saying that.

"BLACK MOON, now what the hell is it?" Arthur Frowned.

"Indeed Arthur, you have the Red moon powers, you are superior powers...you are superiorly powered ONLY AMONG US ..." Richard whines.

"What?" Marcus frustrated asked running his fingers in his hair.

"What do mean by only among us, Dad? come again..." Arthur shook his head in anticipation as if he heard something wrong.

Whereas Olivia and Zenia widen their eyes in shock

"Let me explain," Vincent took the initiative to explain that.

"As we all know, in the magical world the Red Moon powers are the superior one, but in fact, as every coin has two sides."

"The Red Moon Powers are for the good wizards and… The Black Moon Powers are for the Evils."

"What the f***k...? Nobody told this earlier." Marcus frowned punching the table.

"From nobody, you mean Jacob...right?"...Richard asked grinning.

"Yes," Marcus yelled.

"How could he tell you about that. He is a bloody betrayer, a puppet in the hands of Dragons..."Richard's eyes turned red in anger.

"Calm down Richie. it's the time for the real revenge we have to be calm and composed." Henry said rubbing Richard's back making him calm down.

The evil Black Moon powers as a fact are the superior power than Red Moon Powers. Vincent melancholy said.

<u>CHAPTER-37 "ZOHAN's WORRIES"</u>

"Does that mean our Red moon powers are useless? The efforts we made to win them were a waste." Marcus grunted in agony.

"I didn't mean that son," Vincent said patting his hand.

"We can only win over Draco's powers with your Red moon powers," Henry added.

"Okay, I understood...I guess. "Marcus sneered scratching his forehead.

Richard, Henry and Zohan, turn wise turn explained their complete plan.

"Yeah, it's going to be adventurous." Olivia chuckled.

"We will meet again tomorrow, now it's time to leave," Vincent said

"Yes, you must leave the kingdom of the sea before dawn," Zohan demanded.

"Guys let's go back to the Snake kingdom," Vincent demanded raising from her chair.

Everyone hugged each other.

"I want to stay more with you Richie," Vincent said snuggling in his arms.

"Zenia... aren't you coming with us?" Arthur flirtatiously asked,

"What will I do there...? It will be day by the time you reached there," she asked mockingly.

"Ooo... you want night fun." he mocked back.

He leaned over her and kissed her.

"It's time to go...kids," Vincent said cutting them off.

Zenia snapped shyly.

Vincent asked everyone to hold her hand. Olivia hugged her parents before leaving.

Arthur, Marcus, Vincent and Olivia disappeared from the water palace with a spell.

They all appeared in their respective room in the Smith palace,

Olivia looked at the clock its 4:30 am, she was quite tired and feeling sleepy she laid on the bed and soon fell asleep,

Vincent also thought of having rest and asleep.

Arthur and Marcus appeared in Marcus's room.

Both were excited and restless.

"What do you think about the plan Arthur?" Marcus asked changing his clothes.

Arthur was lying on the sofa lost in his thoughts.

"Arthur," Marcus shouted.

Arthur came out of his trance.

"I think the plan is brilliant but I am thinking of Dyna," he responded.

"Dyna the Dragon Princess," Marcus frowned.

"Why are you worried about our enemies daughter?" he asked.

"I am thinking what if he reached you before Olivia." Arthur mocked looking at him.

"Shut up Arthur." Marcus scowls throwing his shirt on him.

"I am just kidding." Arthur huffed shoving the shirt from his face.

"Actually, you make sense, Arthur if it would be Dyna, I would never be able to forgive me," Marcus said sitting next to Arthur.

"Now let's wait for the invitation...yes." both gave a high five.

"You better control your anger and say as you were instructed to do." Arthur seriously ordered Marcus.

"You better behave little one." Marcus chortled.

Arthur flipped his phone and looked at the time it was 5:30 am, "I think we still have some time for a quick nap," Arthur sneered jumping in the bed.

"Won't you change your clothes?" Marcus asked putting on his pyjamas.

"No bro, I am damn lazy for that." Arthur yawned.

"Come let's sleep." Arthur said patting the other side of the bed, Marcus set an alarm for 9 am...sleep, well brother..." Marcus said shrugging in the quilt.

In the Water Palace, Richard and others are happy to reunite their family after long...

Richard was overwhelmed to meet his kids and wife.

"You are indeed a best friend and a wonderful brother. We all are so blessed to have you, Henry." Richard appreciated Henry hugging him tightly.

"I am feeling honoured Richie that I could save you all," Henry responded hugging him tighter.

 Both sob harder in happiness.

"Guys if you are done with this emotional roller coaster ride, it's time to go back to our room, You both should rest now." Lily who was standing beside Henry chuckled.

"Hmm...sure..." Richard hugged Lily.

Henry helped Richard to lay on the bed and both left.

Zenia lying restless on her bed, rolling again and again unable to sleep.

She desperately misses Arthur.

Zenia tried telepathy to contact but she couldn't connect as he was in deep sleep.

Zenia kept rolling on the bed.

Zohan a strong king was quite worried about the plan they just discussed and he was thinking, walking back and forth in his room.

He is worried because in this his granddaughter and grandson's life is at the stake.

He imprisoned Dyna after replacing her with Olivia.

Dyna is still unaware that she has been kidnapped by her grandfather.

"I am sorry darling, Please forgive me, I am doing this to save you and your elder brother. I am doing it for my daughter. She will understand my intentions behind this sin." He was lonely talking to himself.

Zenia couldn't sleep so she decided to go out for a walk. While walking down the corridor she saw Zohan restlessly walking back forth in his room.

"Grandpa..."

Zohan jerked with her voice.

Ohh! Zenia...come in...Zohan said gesturing for her to enter.

"What happened Grandpa? Why do you look so worried?" She asked.

Zenia is staying in the kingdom since a child and has grown a special bond with Zohan as Lily and Rose.

(Zohan's daughter) was best friends,

Zohan remembered the first time Zenia called her Grandpa. He was so happy to hear her calling him grandpa, since then he considers her a dear granddaughter.

"No...nothing like that honey..." he pretended to be calm.

"Come on Grandpa. You know you can't lie to me. just tell me. Is it about Dyna or Lucifer come on spit it up." she demanded.

Zohan heaves a sigh taking a chair to seat.

"Dyna..." he said holding his head.

Zenia takes a seat next to him wrap her arms around his shoulder, comforting him rubbing his arm.

"Will Dyna ever forgive me?" he asked looking into her eyes.

"Of course Grandpa, She will. She has to. I will make sure she does. I will explain everything to her at the right time. She is smart enough to differentiate between the good and the bad. She will certainly choose the good." Zenia confidently answered

"Amen," Zohan Muttered.

"I think you should rest now...you are not well..." Zenia said helping him stand from the chair and put him on the bed.covered him with the quilt.

"Trust me, grandpa...Dyna will love you more and will stay with you forever." She kissed him on his forehead and whispered in his ears.

Zenia stayed there unless Zohan fell asleep.

CHAPTER-38 "DRAGONS"

In the Smith palace at around 9:30 in the morning. Vincent, Arthur and Marcus were casually talking at the Dining table having their breakfast.

Marcus received a call from Tom.

"Master..., someone from the Dragon kingdom is asking for you..."Tom said.

"Send him in," Marcus ordered with a devilish smirk.

Vincent and Arthur understood his expression but couldn't react as Jacob was also there with them.

"Master," Tom politely said bowing to everyone.

"Master, this is Gabriel from the Dragon Kingdom," he said pointing to a tall broad man standing next to him.

"Dragons??"Jacob coughed spitting the food out on his laps.

"Sorry..." Jacob muttered wiping his clothes.

"Easy Jacob," Vincent smirked handing him another tissue paper.

Marcus turned to Gabriel.

"May I know the reason for your arrival, Gabriel," Marcus asked pushing his chair back leaving the dining area.

Marcus moved to the living area. Tom and Gabriel followed him.

He took a seat on a sofa with his arms on the back of the sofa and legs crossed.

Master, I came to invite you on behalf of King Draco. Gabriel said taking a step forward to Marcus offering him a box of chocolates and an invitation card.

Marcus signalled Tom to take the invitation.

Gabriel handed the box and the invitation card to Tom.

"Is there anything else you want to convey?" Marcus ruthlessly asked.

"Nothing Master," Gabriel answered.

Marcus gave a stern look to Tom and Tom walked out with Gabriel.

Jacob excitedly ran towards Marcus.

"Why Dragons invited us?" he asked faking a smile.

"You can read by yourself Uncle," Marcus said glancing at Vincent and Arthur who is sitting at the dining table.

"That's great!" Jacob's eyes widened reading the invitation.

"Anything excited uncle?" Arthur asked walking to them.

Jacob turned to Arthur.

"Yes, King Draco invited us on the occasion of the coronation ceremony of Prince Lucifer coming Monday." His voice is full of happiness.

"Isn't that excited boys?" Jacob asked looking at them both.

"Indeed very excited!" Vincent said.

Everyone turned to her.

She was standing her arms close to her chest.

"Em...Er...Queen." Jacob stammer responding her back.

"Mom..., See what we have, dragon's Prince coronation ceremony invitation." Arthur chuckled.

"I think we should ignore this invitation, I have so many important business meetings to attend," Marcus said throwing away the box.

"We should have considered it," Jacob said.

"Why the hell you want us to consider our enemies invitation uncle?" Marcus yelled.

"I can explain Marcus... at least listen to me before concluding." Jacob insisted.

"I am saying to consider that because I want to know the truth behind your father's death," he explained taking a seat next to Marcus.

"Dragons has no relation to Dad's death..." Marcus said knitting his brows in astonishment.

"Oh, Jesus...how much this moron can fake?" Vincent thought hearing Jacob's words.

"Is Draco responsible for Dad's death?" Arthur asked cutting Jacob.

"No...No!"Jacob frowned.

"Guys you are taking me wrong.

I am saying that this is the right time we should expand our social circle with the wizards.

I know, I was the one who always forced you both to stay away from all the other wizard kings it is because I want you and the Queen to be safe.

Now we have the Queen back and both have grown as mature and responsible adults. Most important you have won the Red Moon powers...We need not be afraid of anyone now. We are strong enough to face any danger. Jacob tried to manipulate and provoke them to consider the Invitation."

Vincent heaves a sigh.

"I think Jacob makes sense. We have to fight our fears and expand our social circle. We can't live in the agony of the past...you should consider the invitation." she said to her sons.

Arthur and Marcus nodded in unison with a grin.

"Fine! then I need to wrap my meeting at the earliest...I have to leave for the company we have only three days left, it is already Friday you see." Marcus said getting out of the living room.

"He needs me for that." Jacob followed with an excuse.

After Marcus and Jacob left.

Vincent and Arthur walked to Olivia.

Arthur entered Olivia's room and was surprised to see Zenia there.

"Hey, what a pleasant surprise," he said kissing Zenia's forehead.

"What's the matter, Zenia? Why are you here?" Vincent asked worriedly.

"Nothing to worry about," Zenia answered wrapping her arm around Vincent's shoulders.

"I am here because..."

"Because she was missing Arthur." Olivia chortled cutting Zenia.

 "Shut up Oliv." Zenia scowls.

Vincent laughed and Arthur's eyes sparkled hearing that.

"Actually, after you, all leave last night. King Zohan was very restless thinking of her granddaughter."

"So, there is a slight change in the plan."

CHAPTER-39 "DYNA"

"King Zohan desired Dyna to attend the coronation," Zenia said.

"But, we have decided that Olivia will attend the coronation disguise as Dyna!." Arthur exclaimed.

"Yes, we decided but unfortunately he changed his mind.today morning Lucifer came to invite grandpa to his coronation ceremony. He promised grandpa to be the kind and honest King."

"King Zohan's heart melts with his words and straight away confess his sin to Dyna in the hollow room,"

"Dyna forgives him as he told him his fair intention behind her kidnap...Now she is also in with us in the plan." Zenia explained.

"WHAAT???"...Arthur yelled in shock.

"Shhhh." Zenia put her finger on his lips to stop him from saying forth.

Zenia Snap her fingers and a beautiful blond hair girl appeared in the room.

"Guys, she is Dyna." Zenia introduced Dyna to everyone.

Everyone was shocked by her sudden appearance.

Arthur arched his eyebrows at Zenia in anxiety.

"Don't worry Arthur she will not harm us. She is our friend as he also wanted her father and brother to be noble and will help us in our revenge." Zenia explained wrapping her arm around Dyna's shoulder.

"Hello everyone," Dyna greeted.

Olivia and Vincent nodded with a smile whereas Arthur faked a smile to her.

"I know it's difficult to trust a villain's daughter, but believe me I am not like him, I never participated in any of his evil deeds. I always worked hard to change his mindset.

Now when I came to know that grandpa also desired Lucifer to change his evil way to conquer the magic world. Grandpa made me understand that my mom never was happy with dad's mindset and she died because of my dad's sin...Now, I want mom to be proud of me. I want her sacrifice to get paid back to her...where ever she is now I want her holy spirit to rest in peace...I just want to do this for my mom...believe me." Dyna tried to convince everyone with her soft and anguish words.

"You can do that alone by your way as well, why you came to join us?" Arthur furiously asked

Vincent pinched Arthur for his harsh words.

"Aouch." Arthur groaned.

"I apologize on his behalf," Vincent said.

"No need to apologize, it's perfectly fine Queen, I can understand because of my dad you all have suffered a lot, I owe you more apologies...Dyna said kneeling, crying in front of Vincent...

Vincent was surprised by his rude behaviour and looked at Arthur.

Arthur gave a curious glance at Zenia as he is unable to understand what drama is going on?

Zenia wink at him and signalled him to be patient.

Vincent holds Dyna from her shoulder and helps her stand back.

"Oh darling, you don't have to do this, it's not your fault, Arthur is a generous boy and never behaved like this with anyone, maybe he is in a state of shock or got confused with all that things happening for a few days. He needs some time to understand.just lend us a day I will make him understand." Vincent said.

"Thank you, Queen." Dyna nodded and hugged Vincent.

Zenia, Olivia and Arthur shared a glance trying to figure out what is going around them,

Whereas Vincent behaved calm and composed talking to Dyna.

Dyna will stay here with you all and she also wants to meet Marcus so that she can spend some time with him to be perfect at the coronation. Zenia said pressing her lips as Olivia gave her a harsh gaze.

Understanding the intensity of the situation. Vincent interferes,

"I think let Dyna meet Marcus at lunch today and leave it on Marcus. What time he will have further scheduled to spend with Dyna? Let me first introduce you to the palace staff." Vincent and Dyna walked out of the room.

Arthur and Olivia were shocked by Vincent words and Zenia tried to control her laugh looking at Arthur and Olivia's mouth wide open in shock.

As soon as they both moved out of the room,

Arthur enchanted the room secure.

"What the hell you just said, Zenia? Did you lost your mind?" He scowls at Zenia.

"Woah Woah!...calm down Arthur...I can explain it." Zenia sneered.

"It is not a joke Zenia..." Olivia growled taking a step close to Zenia.

"Indeed it's not a joke but you guys made it like a joke to me. I didn't expect Arthur to behave like this." Zenia said looking at Arthur.

Arthur squeeze his eyes at her "What? then shall I be happy that you are betraying your sister by putting his fiance with another girl?" he yelled throwing his hands in the air.

"NO, NO...nothing like that if you permit can I say something?" Zenia politely asked.

"Just spit that out Zen," Olivia frowned.

"Ok...please you guys...first of all,"

"Please be calm down," Zenia said handing them a glass of water.

Olivia's eyes are wet in agony, she took the glass with trembling hands.

"We didn't get much time, Zenia hope you understand," Olivia said looking deep into her eyes.

"I know sis, I never thought of anything like that, and I know how deeply you both are in love," Zenia said wrapping her arm around Olivia's shoulder.

CHAPTER-40 "COUPLE'S FIGHT"

"Listen, guys, I can't tell you all in front of Dyna, but I guess Queen being elder understood all by herself that is why she behaved calmly,"

"I am sure Dyna is here as per Dragons planning because I saw her devilish face during her childhood visit to the Kingdom of Sea, she was never so considerate about her mother or her death, she even didn't attend her mother's funeral because of some stupid reasons."

"I saw grandpa crying alone all the time worried about Lucifer and Dyna. Now for the sake of grandpa, we all have to pretend to be nice to her."

"Why she want to get introduced specifically to Marcus?" Olivia frowned cutting Zenia.

"I am not sure about that sister, certainly, I can say that Dyna is not easy to go girl. Did you remember, that Draco planted Dyna as Olivia to fall in love with Marcus? I guess, she is still on that plan and wanted to get married to Marcus."

A tear rolled out of Olivia's eyes as Zenia's words just stabbed her heart.

"Hey, Don't worry Marcus only loves you. I can assure you that." Arthur consoled wiping her tears.

"I never had my family with me because of Draco and now his daughter is here to fetch away my love and you want me to be calm," Olivia said sobbing.

"Oliv, do you think, we all will let her do anything like this to you? Don't you have trust in Marcus and your love?" Zenia asked holding Olivia's hands.

"I didn't forgive him...he kept asking me and apologizing to me but I being so stubborn Didn't accept he apologizes, even didn't admit my love to him and now I am afraid that Dyna will be the beneficiary of my stupidity." Olivia kept crying.

"Never ever," Arthur yelled "I know my brother, he is not a womanizer that any woman can have him.

He gave you his virginity and will be in love with you and only you Olivia...have some trust in him, no matter you forgive him or not, he will keep apologizing until his last breath. "Arthur sternly said.

"I have trust in him but I am afraid of losing him," Olivia said sobbing.

"Listen, Olivia, you have to be strong this time and have to control your jealous factor. I understand it is very difficult for us to see our love with other girls but believe me, sis, we all are with you and Marcus will love you and only you...nobody can ever snatch him away...NOT EVEN THAT DRAGON GIRL." Zenia confidently exclaimed.

"Let Dyna try her luck on Marcus and let Marcus show his true love for you, take this situation as your love exam sis." Zenia chuckled.

"Yes, I think you guys are correct. I need not worry. "Olivia firmly said wiping her tears.

"Now we all are in on this." Zenia joined hands with Arthur and Olivia.

"Let's discuss the plan," Arthur said.

Vincent while showing Dyna the Smith Mansion Vincent kept checking her reactions.

In a span of an hour, Dyna asked numerous times about Marcus.

"Marcus will be back soon," Vincent said.

As Vincent completed her sentence she saw Marcus walking in the main door.

"Speak of the devil and devil is here," Vincent chortled pointing towards Marcus.

Dyna turned towards him and blushed to see a tall handsome boy in a black tuxedo...her eyes stopped on his deep blue sparkling eyes and his enchanting smile made her fall more for him.

She tightly clenched her hands in fist controlling her dirty desires to come out so soon.

"Hey Son, come here," Vincent shouted from the corner of the living room. Marcus who was busy talking on the phone didn't notice them and turned to Vincent's voice.

"I will call you back." saying that he disconnected the call and walked towards his mother.

Marcus gave a tiny glance at Dyna and then hugged his mom.

"Hey, mom...how are you doing?"

"I am doing good darling," Vincent said patting his back.

"Who is this beautiful guest mom?" Marcus flirtatiously asked.

Dyna's face got cover with pink dust all over by Marcus's voice.

"Ohh..hmm, let me take the honour to introduce Dyna, Princess Kingdom Dragons." Vincent chuckled.

Marcus widened his eyes hearing Dragon's Princess.

"What is she doing here mom?" he whispered in her ear.

"Dyna is here to spend some time with us, especially with you.so that we can all attend Lucifer's coronation as per the plan," Vincent said winking.

"Marcus got a hint about something fishy is here but he behaves very calm as he trusts Vincent if she is behaving calmly it means the situation is under control and in our favour." he thought...

"Marcus, Why don't you take Dyna out for a lunch date?" Vincent modestly said.

"L...Lun...lunch date..." Marcus stammer in shock at Vincent's words.

"Yes, I would love that." Dyna bluntly said.

"Mom, you know I have a very busy schedule and I am totally swamped with my meetings. I came back home because I have another meeting at a nearby cafe." Marcus trying to excuse.

"That's fine Marcus. I won't disturb you in your meeting and we can have lunch or coffee later." Dyna sweetly said winking at him.

"Mom." Marcus frowned.

Vincent gave Marcus an orderly gaze and he just nodded.

"What the hell is going on? Will someone gonna tell me?" Marcus asked mind linking with Arthur and Vincent.

Before Arthur could respond. Vincent said "Do as I said" and distorted the link.

Marcus felt so helpless and feeling guilty of cheating on Olivia.

<u>CHAPTER-41 "LUNCH DATE"</u>

Marcus down-heartedly walked out of the mansion with Dyna.

"So how's your business going on?" Dyna suddenly asked breaking the weird silence among them.

"em..er.. fine," Marcus replied.

Marcus as a gentleman opened the car door for Dyna and took the side seat.

"Nora's Cafe," he ordered the driver.

Dyna shyly sitting beside him often stealing glances at him.

Marcus nervously kept running his fingers in his hair, fidgeting with his mobile. Olivia in his mind making him more worried about how to face her.

Suddenly his phone rang and his eyes widened to see the caller.

"Mom," he murmured.

"yes m... "he answered the call with trembling hands.

"Marcus be-careful with Dyna and behave well. I want her to be happy and comfortable with you." Vincent ordered him.

"But mom, how can I? Oli."

"Do as I said, Marcus? " Vincent disconnected the call.

He faked a smile to Dyna and felt strange about his mother's changed behaviour,

Maybe Dyna is Mom's best friend daughter that is why she wants me to behave well with her but what's her purpose in sending me on this lunch date? Date...rubbish... I only want to date my Oliv always and forever... he blushed thinking about Olivia.

What... did I say to my Oliv? She didn't even forgive me. Will she accept me? This drive was never so long. he thought frustratedly looking out of the window.

The driver pushed the breaks ..." we reached Nora's cafe Master," he informed.

"Oh yes," Marcus huffed heaving a relaxed sigh.

"hmm...Ok...Dyna I have a small meeting with my clients and I will try to finish it as soon as possible...hope you won't mind." Marcus asked walking into the cafe.

"No, not at all." Dyna shyly replied.

"That's great," He said faking a smile.

"Master...Mr.Taylor is here!" Fin who already reached the cafe for preparations informed Marcus.

"Fin, she is Dyna. She is my guest here so please take good care of her." Marcus ordered to Fin.

Fin nodded.

"Dyna, make yourself comfortable and enjoy the ambience...I will join you soon. hope you don't mind?" Marcus courteously asked.

"Never mind, I can wait." Dyna sweetly answered.

"Excuse me I have to go," Marcus said and moved to his reserved table for the meeting.

Fin took Dyna to the other table quite away from Marcus's table.

"Miss, you can order whatever you would like to have?" Fin asked.

"Just a coffee." She replied.

A waiter immediately served her a coffee.

Fin stood near the table taking care of Dyna.

"Mr.Fin...How long does the meeting will go?"...Dyna asked sipping her coffee.

"I regret to say. I have no idea about that." Fin politely answered.

"Is this Marcus's favourite cafe?"

"Yes, Miss...Master, like to visit this cafe...he likes the peaceful atmosphere and beautiful decor of this place."

"hmm, I see." she smouldered looking around.

"What else he likes the most?" she sweetly asked.

He spends most of his time in company and business.

"Tell me things other than business?" she ruthlessly asked.

He likes to play golf sometimes.

"Does he have a girlfriend?" she asked arching an eyebrow.

"Emm...sorry...Miss...I don't know his personal affairs." Fin shocked to hear that question.

"What kind of girls does he like?" she asked.

"Actually, I don't know what kind of girls, Master like but, he hates girls who latch around him." Fin nonchalantly answered.

Fin looked at his watch.

Dyna looks around at the surrounding.

It is not an ordinary cafe. It's not less than a luxurious restaurant with very few visitors.

The highly maintained staff and the soft music that rolled around is wonderful to calm your nerves. She kept observing, Fin and steal glances at Marcus's table.

Marcus is engrossed deeply in his meeting that he completely forgets about Dyna. An hour later he wrapped the meeting and was about to leave the cafe.

"Master..." Fin called.

Marcus turned to his voice and Jerked to see Dyna waiting for him.

"Ohhh shit." He muttered scratching his forehead. How could I forget about this new trouble?

He slowly walked to Dyna's table, Fin grabbed a chair for him.

"I regret you waited so long for me," Marcus said faking a smile.

"No problem," she said blushing.

"Hope Fin took good care of yours?" he asked looking at Fin.

"Certainly, he does!" she huffed.

"Fin go through this file once and send me the report by evening. Now you can leave and call me if you need anything." Marcus said handing him the file.

Fin Nodded and left.

"So...have you ordered something for you Dyna?" he asked looking down the menu.

"I had coffee." she winks tiredly.

"You must try their grilled fish...the chef cooks the world's best fish."

"Ok" she agreed, pressing her lips.

Marcus orders the food.

"So, tell me how can I reimburse your time loss?" he flirtatiously asked faking a smile.

"Well...I can say ... let's tour around the city," she meticulously demanded.

"SURE, why not?" he said pressing his lips.

"Your order sir." the waiter said while putting the tray of grilled fish on the table.

"mmmm....this food smells awesome," Dyna said sniffing the bowl.

"Yes, let's taste," Marcus said serving her.

Their lunch went well with small talks.

After the lunch as demanded Dyna asked him for the city tour...

Sure...Marcus said shrugging his shoulders.

Marcus took her to various places and she spends a good time, her plan is going well so far.

"Marcus, I must say, it was the best day, I ever spent. Thank you." Dyna said giving an ear to ear grin.

"Pleasure is always mine, princess," Marcus replied.

"So what's more about your city?" Dyna asked looking out of the window.

Marcus phone ranged..."Excuse me." he excused Dyna and answered the call.

"OK," he said and disconnected the call.

"Let's go to one more place," he said accelerating the car.

"Where are we going?" Dyna asked.

"Surprise...who will surely be going to like that place? he said rolling the wheel."

"Okay,"

Marcus drive in the parking of a tall building.

"Hope you don't have any meeting again. If that's the scene...so kindly excuse me." Dyna dramatically said.

"Not at all." Marcus pushed the break and came out of his car.

"Both walked to an elevator and Marcus swiped his floor card...the elevator paces up to the building.

Dyna was amused to see his office and his style of working.

"So Miss, Did you like this place?" Marcus asks flirtatiously.

"Yesss, I loved it...I never saw a young, dynamic boss." She said smouldering.

"You are not only a good guide, but a handsome boy also...you are indeed a perfect businessman, Marcus." She smirked appreciating him.

"Thanks, Dyna and I never heard so much appreciation." he chuckled...both laughed at this.

Marcus ordered some snacks for them. Dyna enjoyed being with Marcus, whereas Marcus is constantly worried about Olivia in his head.

CHAPTER-42 "HEARTBREAKING"

In the evening Marcus and Dyna came back home.

Everyone was enjoying their evening tea in the garden.

Dyna deliberately pretends to fall and Marcus held from her waist preventing her to fall.

Which Olivia saw and her heart twitched with the scene.

Sadness pondered in her eyes.

Arthur who was sitting beside Olivia was also in shock, but he couldn't react and patted Olivia's hand ."Don't worry...it happens," he whispered trying to console Olivia.

"Hmm," Olivia controlled her emotions and casually kept sipping her tea ignoring Marcus.

Dyna understood Olivia jealousy and she deliberately links her arms with Marcus.

"Hello everyone." Marcus greeted.

"Hey, Dyna so how was your date with my son?" Vincent chuckled.

On hearing that...Arthur coughed spitting his tea. "Date?" He screamed.

Olivia patted his back..." don't worry, It happens," She mocked handing him a tissue.

"Excuse me, I have to make an urgent call," Marcus said looking at Olivia and Arthur.

Marcus felt embarrassed, he couldn't bear Olivia's sad eyes and walked to his room.

"Excuse me ladies I need to clean myself." Arthur also walked out.

"Hey bro, wait for me...I want to talk," Arthur screamed running behind Marcus.

Marcus stopped and turned to his voice.

"I know Arthur, what you want to ask, it's not at all a date. I don't know, what's wrong with mom, why she is behaving so weird. I am already feeling embarrassed and bad about Olivia...so please don't start anything." Marcus frustratedly spat running his fingers in his hair.

"Chill bro," Arthur said wrapping his arm around Marcus's shoulder.

"I also don't know what mom is up to...but definitely, something big gonna happen soon," Arthur chuckled.

"Hey, Arthur, tell me why Dyna is here? Why do I need to spend time with her? I am so confused and the time I just spend with her is just because of mom." Marcus said walking into his room.

"Well...Zenia who brought Dyna here told me that Dyna will accompany you on Lucifer's coronation instead of Olivia."

"What the hell are you talking and why didn't nobody informed me about that?" Marcus screamed smashing his phone on the floor in anger.

Arthur's eyes rolled down to the smashed phone and he gave an awful grin and he understood Marcus embarrassment that is turning into anger... it was all because he can't replace anyone with Olivia.

"Great." he chortled.

"I mean you are still the same angry bird bro..." he laughed.

"Arthur I am serious...you even can't feel what embarrassment I am going through...Olivia still couldn't forgive and even after what has happened today I am losing hope." Marcus said holding his head.

"Olivia loves you, bro." Arthur sneered.

"What? come again." Marcus said raising his brows.

"Yes, you heard it right. She loves you when she heard about you and Dyna she broke down and admit her love for you in front of us."

"It's your love exam bro you have to earn her forgiveness...you should play fair and win her back."

Dyna is not easy to go girl...Zenia told us she is here with a hidden purpose and I am sure her hidden purpose is "YOU,"

"MEEE"...Marcus was shocked to hear that.

"Yes, you remember dad told us that. they deliberately replace Olivia with Dyna."

Dyna wants you and only you.

Zenia also told me that Dyna is with us in destroying the Dargon's Crown but she is not sure of her inner devilish will.

"Now I made a plan. You have to pretend to love Dyna and made her admit her devilish desire to you, then only we can easily destroy the crown and can win over the dragons and the Draco."

"NO, Arthur, I can't even think of any other girl...Olivia will never forgive me after that." Marcus said gritting his teeth.

"Bro it's the right time to take revenge and Dyna is here to distract you from our plan,"...Arthur tried to convince him.

"Ok listen, Marcus, you have to pretend, you have to play this bluff bro...tell me, don't you want our dad to be back at his palace."

"Don't you want uncle Henry to get back his kingdom?" Moreover don't you want to marry Olivia?

Arthur smouldered.

"I need some time to think," Marcus said.

"We don't' have time bro, Only four days left for the coronation."

Dyna will stay here with us and she will always latch around you trying to fetch you away from Olivia and you have to make sure that her plan is going inflow.

Then only we get to know what's her true intention, "Is she truly with us or she is as evil as Draco?"

"We will not let history repeat." Arthur roared.

"How...how can I do that?" Marcus again asked in anger.

"You can bro,"

"I never felt so helpless Arthur...never ever," Marcus screamed hugging Arthur.

"You have to be strong bro.. it is about all of us." Now only you and you can save us.

"It's just a matter of few days bro." Dyna will be coming to you any moment just be prepared to pretend...Arthur said...

"Hmm.. you're right...I need to shower first, I need to calm down my nerves." Marcus said wiping his face with his hands.

"Can you do me a favour, Arthur?"... He asked.

"Tell me." Arthur answered...

"Tell Olivia...She is my life, and I only love her." Marcus words were full of affection.

"Sure bro..she will be happy to hear that." Arthur smiled.

"Thanks...just leave me alone for a moment Arthur," Marcus said walking towards his bathroom.

"Bye, bro, Take care." Arthur waved him with a smile and left.

Marcus frustratedly put off his clothes and soaked himself in a cold water bathtub to calm down his nerves and anger.

He closed his eyes and trying to sense Olivia.

He saw her playing with Alice in the garden.

"I love you, Olivia," he muttered.

Knock..knock...

He came out of his trance with the knock at his door.

"Marcus are you there?" Dyna asked...

Marcus smashed his hands in water in anger.

"Yes, wait, Dyna," he replied.

He hurriedly came out of bathroom wearing a towel covering his lower half.

Dyna blushed to see his wet hair and his exposed toned, well build wet chest which is more than enough for her lusty desire to come out.

Marcus deliberately came out like this.

Marcus grin with her response...

She slowly walked to him and started running her fingers on his wet chest.

Marcus hated her touch and couldn't resist that.

He slowly shoved her hands and looked into her eyes.

Her lust can be easily read.

"Do you need something Dyna?" he asked.

"You," she smouldered.

"Really?" he replied.

"You are so young, handsome, smart and..., I am not at all ashamed to say that,

"I fall in love with you the first time I saw you in the morning and now you arose my desires to have you even more," she said shamelessly wrapping her arms around his neck.

Marcus pulled her closed to him clutching her waist.

His warm breath fans her pink cheeks turning them red in heat to have him.

She pressed her lips against him and pushed herself on him, she deepens the kiss closing her eyes, it was so sudden that Marcus couldn't even think or react.

Olivia entered the room and was shocked to see them kissing.

"Oohhh...sorry...sorry," Olivia shocked to see them and immediately shut the door and went out crying with her broken heart.

CHAPTER-43 "CONFESSION"

"Stop!" Marcus said in a low and steady voice.

"Why are you so much in hurry Dyna? I think we should...we should spend some more time together before. Before...before getting closer." He said taking a step away from her.

"But, I don't' think so," Dyna replied taking a step forward to him.

Sniffing her lust Marcus treads towards his wardrobe, and took a pair of black jeans and a white slim-fit V-neck t-shirt to wear.

Dyna half laid on his bed continuously stare at him...licking her lips...

Marcus threw the towel on the chair and put on the jeans.

He then moved to his dressing mirror and started brushing his hair.

"I must say you look dashing in every attire. Handsome," Dyna complimented lazily walking to him.

Marcus gave her a grin and "you look disgusting saying me that," he said in his head.

"So tell me, How and when can we start our relation?" Dyna seductively asked standing close to the mirror.

Marcus frowned with her words and smashed the hairbrush on the floor. Dyna jerked...

"SSSSoorry, if I said something wrong." she panicked.

"Control Marcus," he said to himself again and pretended to be normal.

"Ohh N..No..Nothing like I just hate this hairbrush...so I just broke it," he said turning to her.

"I think Dyna you should go and have some rest you must be tired. I will take you to our lake for boating tomorrow." he threw a fake promise just to get rid of Dyna.

"I am not at all tired, if you say then we can go right now. I love boating and with you spending alone time is my dream." She demanding rolling her fingers on his cheeks.

"hmm..." he slowly shoved her hands from his cheeks as his skin is burning in flames of irritation with her touch.

He softly twists her wrist making her turn back, her back touched his chest. She moaned in pleasure and pain.

She arched her neck pushing her hair from her shoulder exposing her naked back and shoulder,

Her backless dress is very revealing to arose the tempt of any man.

Marcus slightly turned on with her beauty and subconsciously he runs his fingers from his naked shoulder to her naked back...making her moan louder.

"Ohh Marcus,"...she moaned his name.

"Someone is really having majestic moments." Vincent chuckled entering the room.

"Mom." he scoffs.

Marcus pushed Dyna away from him.

Dyna shyly winks, fidgeting with her fingers.

"Dyna, darling I was thinking of taking you to your room," Vincent said grabbing Dyna's hand.

"My room...Can't I stay with Marcus?" Dyna shamelessly asked.

"You can but I think if you will stay with him...he won't let you sleep." Vincent chortled.

"I love that," Dyna muttered.

"Mom," Marcus scoffs again.

"Mom, Dyna is actually tired and I request you please feel free to take her. I have some other important work to finish."

Marcus demanded widening his eyes.

Dyna was shocked to see the sudden change in his behaviour. He is exactly the same mysterious boy I always wondered. She thought smirking.

Vincent took Dyna to her room.

Marcus immediately teleported himself to Olivia's room.

"Oliv..." she called her name but she was nowhere in the room.

Marcus frowned and immediately went to Arthur's room.

"Arthur have you seen Olivia?" he asked ferociously.

"Yeah, she is with Zenia," he replied.

"Is she fine?" Marcus asked.

"Yes, she is perfectly fine," Arthur replied.

"What happened bro, why are you so worried about her?" Arthur asked crossing his arms close to his chest and looking at him with a naughty smirk.

"Emm....Er...unfortunately she saw me and Dyna kissing," Marcus said frustratingly running his hands in his hair.

"Oohh...that's indeed gross." Arthur chuckled.

"I know." Marcus scoffed.

"Don't worry bro...she is mature enough to understand what is going around and she is also fine with whatever you do in order to vanish the dragons," Arthur said handing a glass of wine to him

"Really...?" he curiously asked taking the glass.

"Yes, perhaps the scene does hurt her but she later understood and calmed down," Arthur said sipping the wine.

"I wish I could explain everything to her by myself." Marcus saddened.

"Don't worry bro, it's just a matter of few more days and then everything will go smoothly and WE WILL BE WITH OUR LOVELY WIVES MINGLING ENJOYING OUR HONEYMOON." Arthur loudly sneered.

Marcus smiled with his words and finished his drinks, "Can I have some more wine?" Marcus asked.

"Sure, bro... you can," Arthur poured more wine in their glasses.

"Do you know Arthur? I never felt so pissed off even not when I was attacked by the crocs in the maze. But that filthy girl DYNA, she is so onto me all the day...and there was a time just a few minutes back I actually almost drawn to her beauty...thanks to mom who appeared to save me committing another sin."

"Damn, I am missing Olivia so much... I wish I could get some time with her," he said randomly gulping wine.

"I understand bro!" Arthur said rubbing Marcus's arm.

"You soon will get time together bro...don't worry."

"I want this time to fly as fast as it can," Marcus said smashing the glass on the floor.

A loud voice of glass breaking echoed in the room.

Zenia and Olivia hiding inside the wardrobe immediately came out.

Olivia tightly hugged Marcus..."I am sorry Marcus...I misunderstood you...I am sorry...You are the best person I ever met...I love you and I trust You." Olivia said randomly kissing him all over his face.

"I am sorry too Oliv." Marcus said kissing harder on her lips.

Zenia and Arthur looked at each other with a relaxing smile on their face.

Arthur gives a peck on Zenia's lips...thanking her for her help,

"Ok guys...I think we should leave you alone before you make your babies in front of us." Zenia chortled taking Arthur out of the room.

Marcus and Olivia drifted in each other's love didn't hear and continued making out.

CHAPTER-44 "READY"

Zenia and Arthur are very happy about Olivia and Marcus's patch up.

"Zen,"

"hmm..."

"Let's go for a walk. I also want to spend some time talking to you." Arthur said.

"Sure...I would love that...It's been so long we haven't spent time together." She asked.

"True!" Both walked to the garden for a walk.

"Zenia, there are lot many questions bombarding in my head since Dyna came in." Arthur seriously said.

"I can understand your curiosity, Arthur." Zenia politely replied.

"Dyna is still not aware of dad and Uncle Richard's presence in the Sea Kingdom and moreover she only knows me as her second cousin as King Zohan initially introduced us."

"She never bothers to enquire more about that and now I introduced Olivia as my sister and Queen Vincent as her foster mother, which she didn't consider interested, her only focus to be here is Marcus and she will only and only try to get his love and later marrying him."

"But for us, she is just a source of information about Lucifer and Draco,"

"They surely have planned something big to attack us for sure."

"How can you be sure about that Zen?" Arthur curiously asked cutting her.

"Not only me, in fact, Dad and Richie Uncle is also sure about that."

"We all are sure about this because Draco will never ever invite his biggest enemy ever to be part of his happy moments, After the attack, he lost his powers, paused his desire of conquering the world of magic because of Dad and Aunt Vincent."

"Precisely, he knows that now you both own the Red Moon powers, one of the Ultimate powers,"

"Dyna is pretending to help us, but whole-heartedly she will remain a dragon,"

"What say?" she chuckled.

"Hmm, I think you make sense." Arthur responded scratching his temple.

"Ohh, my doctor lover, there are a lot many complicated things other than science." she chortled pinching his nose.

"Yes, my smart girl," he said pulling her closer.

Both smiled looking into each other's eyes.

"Listen, Arthur, now you have to make sure that Marcus will play his role perfectly, we can't afford to lose Dyna's trust."

"I will take care of Olivia," she affirmed.

"Apparently, they are the one who is suffering the most in this critical strategy...I will surely take care of him," Arthur said going back to the Palace.

"Ok Love, it's time for me to leave, it is not safe to stay here for long, danger all around," Zenia said rolling her eyes around,

"No, I won't let you go." Arthur frowned clenching her hand tightly.

"Arthur don't be so impatient, I am observing that since I admitted my love to you, you were not the same calm and composed Doctor Arthur,"

"Indeed you become a more impatient and stubborn teenage boy...which I don't like." She said shrinking her nose.

"Is it?" Arthur chuckled.

"Yes, It is!" she said cuddling him.

"I love you Zenia and living away from you is something I can't be patient about," Arthur said hugging her tightly.

"Love you too Arthur." Zenia responded shrugging into his arms.

"Ohk...honey, have to go now? See you soon," Zenia said slightly pushing him away.

Arthur kissed her softly and she disappeared with a snap.

Arthur slept in Marcus room as his room was occupied by the lovebirds.

The Next Morning,

Olivia woke up in Marcus's arms. Olivia looked at Marcus's calm face. She never saw him so calm before.

"Is he really that rude, ruthless Master?" she thought,

Marcus felt her gaze on him and he woke up.

Olivia was laying with her chin resting on his chest and eyes on his face.

"Good morning Love..." he said in a groggy voice.

"Good morning," she replied...

Marcus looked at the window and sun rays pouring in the room through the curtains.

"Oliv...I...I..." he didn't find a word to say.

"I trust you, Marcus!" Olivia said looking deep into his eyes cupping his face in her hands.

"Thank you, sweet heart" he said kissing her forehead.

"Always remember one thing Oliv, I love you and only you, whatever you will be going to see or hear about me and Dyna is just the part of our mission nothing personal...hope you understand?" Marcus said wrapping his arms around her.

"I understand...I agree it's quite difficult for me to digest all that I see yesterday was bizarre but after I heard you confessing your emotions, I get to understand how much you love me and your family." Olivia replied.

"Will you forgive now?" he asked looking into her brown eyes.

"I already did that way before?" she answered boring her eyes into his deep blue eyes.

"I love you, Olivia, I can't live without you anymore." He said pulling her into his arms.

"Now, it is time for you to leave before Dyna can come here looking for you." Olivia said pushing him out of the bed.

"Yeah..yeah... it is too much difficult to leave you like that." he said with a long face.

"Don't be sad, all the very best for your mission Honey," Olivia softly said giving him a thumbs up.

"Honey....???did I heard correct...???" he asked widening his eyes.

She shyly nodded.

He put on his t-shirt and leaned over her push his lips on her and the soft kiss turned into a passionate one... after a while, Olivia pushed him away and both laid beside each other gasping and panting heavily.

"Get out of the room," she chortled raising her hand towards the door.

CHAPTER-45 "DAY OF CORONATION"

The next four days.

Marcus remains busy with Dyna and business meetings, therefore, he didn't get any time to meet Olivia.

He spent his day with the clients and was swamped in the company events, in the evening Dyna always latches around so unwillingly he has to ignore Olivia. During dinners, he gets to see her only while dining together stealing glances.

Dyna always stays with him when he is at home. Olivia also didn't give much attention to their PDA's.

Dyna meticulously working on her plans so does the Smith's.

DAY OF CORONATION

Finally, the day has come, the day everyone desperately waited for.

Marcus looks damn handsome in his black tuxedo and Dyna dressed as stunning as she can in her black fishtail backless dress, her hairdo was also stylish, the perfect blonde curls and beautifully blended makeup actually made this vamp looks like an angel today. Olivia was cursing Dyna in her thoughts looking at them walking down the stairs hand in hand.

"YOU GUYS LOOK SO PERFECT TOGETHER." Olivia taunted curling her lips.

Marcus faked a smile, whereas Dyna blushed with her words winking at Marcus.

"I think we should leave," Marcus asked Dyna.

"Won't you wait for us bro?" Arthur loudly asked from the other end of the stairs.

Everyone turned to his voice...

"OH MY GOD..." Olivia giggled in surprise.

She hurriedly climbed up the stairs to reach Arthur and Zenia.

Arthur is wearing a dark blue tuxedo matching the colour of his eyes and Zenia.

"Zenia you are looking so hot...so beautiful...so awesome," Olivia said swirling Zenia giving a 360 degree few of her dresses.

She is wearing a royal blue shimmer off-shoulder body-hugging dress, her silver danglers swinging over her shoulders and the high bun with a silver shimmery butterfly clip at the side of the bun giving her a mesmerizing look.

"YOU GUYS ARE ACTUALLY LOOKING GORGEOUS!" she squealed looking at Marcus and Dyna's face.

"Indeed they are!" Marcus muttered...Dyna elbowed him for saying that...

"AOUCH,..." he grunts.

The three of them came down close to Marcus and Dyna.

"Let us leave now, we are running late." Marcus frowned looking at Olivia's disappointed expressions.

"Yes, sure." Zenia wrapped her hand around Arthur's arm and so does Dyna did to Marcus.

"Take care," Olivia whispered in Zenia's ear.

"Yes, I do...You too take care sis," she said waving at her.

Both the couples disappeared enchanting a spell.

Olivia walked to Vincent's room to calm her nerves...

She knocked at the door "Come in," ... Vincent Softly called her in.

"Queen, Can I stay with you for some time." Olivia sadly asked.

"Yes, honey, you can," Vincent said patting beside the vacant seat.

Both starting talking.

On the other hand

IN THE KINGDOM DRAGON.

The whole palace was beautifully decorated with flowers, globe string lamps, statuesque vases, geometrical vases, perfect sitting arrangements, food stalls all over, hundreds of waiters serving the guests.

"It's indeed a Majestic Coronation Ceremony" Marcus, Zenia, and Arthur were amused to see ceremony decorations. Dyna, on the other hand, seems very happy, her eyes sparkled looking around the palace. She is back at her palace after 3 months.

Lucifer walked the velvet runner pushing Draco's wheelchair.

"Ladies and gentlemen, it is my immense pleasure to Welcome our former King, KING DRACO with his successor and our new king KING LUCIFER." Minister of the kingdom announced.

Everyone applauded giving them a standing ovation.

Marcus and Arthur also applauded pretending to be happy.

Dyna happily ran to her brother and father.

"DAD," she screamed and hugged him leaning over his chair.

"Oh, Dyna... my daughter... it's so good to see you." Draco chuckled kissing her forehead.

"Hey, Lucifer." Dyna hugged him.

"Hey, sis...I missed you so much." He said caressing her hair.

"Dad, I must say the arrangements are wonderful," she said rolling her eyes all over.

"Thank you, princess." He giggled.

Three of them started proceeding towards the huge golden stage for the coronation ceremony...

"Lucifer, If you don't mind can I take dad to the stage," Dyna said clenching the wheelchair's arm.

"Of course!" Lucifer replied giving her access to the wheelchair.

"Dad, Is everything under control?" Dyna whispered.

"Yes," Draco responded.

"How about the snake princes?" he asked.

"Marcus is completely under my influence, he will not be going to harm you. I enchanted his wand." She said smirking devilishly.

"Stupid girl...his wand cannot be enchanted with your powers...he has THE RED MOON POWERS" in his wands." he scowls.

"I know dad but he can't use THE RED MOON POWERS against his love." she chuckled,

"Love??" he frowned.

"Yes, love, dad..., I am not that much stupid, that you think...Marcus is madly in love with me," she kept pushing his wheelchair slowly waving and smiling at the guest...

Lucifer arrogantly walking down the aisle with his family.

His royal attire and ruthless glare exposing him is an evil heart.

Three of them finally reached the centre of the stage waving and greeting their guests.

'WITH DUE PERMISSION OF OUR KING DRACO, I WOULD LIKE TO START THE CORONATION OF HIS LOVING SON AND OUR CHARMING PRINCE...PRINCE LUCIFER.' the minister again announces.

The whole kingdom echoed with applause and cheers...

A huge golden crown appeared in the air, flying over the crowd towards the stage, everyone raised their heads in amusement looking at the crown, rolling their eyeballs in the direction of the crown.

The crown stopped near King Draco with the action of his hand.

"Today, I KING DRACO BLACK ATKINSON, proud to announce my loving son Lucifer Draco Atkinson the new king of the dragons." he arrogantly announced raising his hands towards the crown.

He asked Lucifer to come forward to him.

"Dad, wait." Lucifer scoffs.

"Why?" Draco growled...

"Grandpa...where is grandpa Zohan?" Lucifers asked looking around the guests.

"He must be busy with other guests."

"Don't waste time let's do it." Draco scowled.

"No, dad without grandpa, I will not have your crown." Lucifer scoffs.

"Stop being ridiculous Lucifer," Draco said gritting his teeth,

"GRANDPA...where are you?" Lucifer screamed.

Zohan appeared on the stage from nowhere.

"Grandpa..." Lucifer eyes sparkled with his presence.

"I want my coronation to be done by you," Lucifer expressed his desire.

Draco was shocked to hear his words.

"Lucifer," he growled.

"DAD, please...I promised him that, please let me be at my promise." Lucifer pleaded, kneeling down.

Draco looked at Dyna in anticipation but Dyna nodded pressing his shoulder.

"Dyna you too." he scoffs.

"Dad, Grandpa is our elder and we should give him this privilege as a token of respect," Dyna said.

Draco was shocked by the sudden changes in his children behaviours.

"Is this their scrupulous plan?" He asked himself.

He was confusedly looking at Dyna and Lucifer.

CHAPTER-46 "LUCIFER'S MOURN"

Draco thought for a while and everyone was also shocked to see this family drama of the dragons. Everyone started whispering.

Draco looking at the guest disturbing expressions, unwillingly handed the crown to his father-in-law faking a smile.

"You win father-in-law fetching my children," Draco said gritting his teeth in anger.

Zohan took a step forward and takes the crowns from Draco's hands...his eyes glowered looking at the sparkling crown.

He raised the crown over Lucifer's head, Lucifer slightly leans his head so that Zohan can put on the crown on his head.

Zohan looked at Dyna. Dyna nodded smirking.

Zohan grins and he slightly raised the crown towards Lucifer's head.

Draco pulse was increasing with every moment of the crown.

"Do it fast, you old man." Draco impatiently shouted.

Zohan looked at Draco, his face turned red in anger...

He moved the crown slightly more closer to Lucifer's head.

Everyone cheering, chuckling and applauding.

Zohan turned his gaze to everyone and slightly raised the crown towards Lucifer's head.

Everyone was stunned to see Zohan hands.

Zohan with a wink put the crown on his own head.

"What the hell?" Draco growled.

Lucifer was shocked to see Zohan turning into Marcus.

Dyna smirk and pushed Draco's wheelchair with full force towards Lucifer, before Lucifer and Draco could understand Draco fall from the wheelchair over Lucifer, both fall on the ground.

Arthur and Zenia also appeared on the stage. Lucifer tried to hold Draco, balancing himself to stand again.

"Dynaa...are you out of your mind?" Lucifer's scowls gasping.

"Sorry ..come again." Dyna chortled and turned into Olivia.

Draco and Lucifer astonishingly looking at her.

Arthur and Marcus raised their wands towards the crown and enchanted a spell, the crown burst into pieces with a loud blast and flames all over.

Draco grunts in pain his body started burning like his crown.

"You can't do this to me, you snakes," Draco growled grunting.

"Dad...dad." Lucifer trying to save Draco by enchanting spells and raising his wands on him, over and over, again to save Draco but all his efforts are in vain.

Arthur enchants a spell and raised his wands at burning Draco and the flames went off with his spell.

Draco understood this is his end... end of his life...his evil deeds. He grunts in pain...gasping...

Zohan, Richard, Henry, Lily and Dyna also appeared on the stage.

"Grandpa, Dyna...you betrayed us," Lucifer screamed putting burnt Draco on his laps.

"No Lucifer...we didn't...this is the fruit of Draco's evil deed," Zohan responded.

"You...Cowards!" Draco grunts and shockingly looked at Henry and Richard.

"Draco this is your end, devilish end!" Richard exclaimed.

"Dad...dad...No!" Dyna crouched near Draco, drenched in tears.

"Dad..., please admit your sins, please let your soul to release peacefully,"

"What are you saying, Dyna?" Lucifer scowls.

"Yes,... he is our dad... who destroyed many kingdoms, killed many innocent wizards and their families in his life."

"Lucifer..., dad never met an accident, he lost his legs because of his killing spell counter-attacked him, the killing spell he enchants on the king of snakes to kill him," Dyna explained.

"Stop it, Dyna..." Lucifer huffs...

"I know brother it's very difficult to digest but believe me...he is the one who killed our mom to conquer the kingdom of the sea," Dyna said sobbing harder.

"I already forgave you, dad. Now please admit your deeds to Lucifer, he trusts you and only you. Mom always loved you and you betrayed him, you always betrayed us, it's so shameful dad you betrayed your own blood ingest of conquering the world of magic...but dad nothing is forever...nothing...you destroyed yourself as well..she sobs harder."

"Dad..., ignore her..., I won't let you go..., Dad.., You are my only ideal, my god, my world." tears kept rolling down his eyes.

Draco was completely broken by his son's tear.

"Lucifer...I can't be anyone's ideal," he grunts in pain.

Lucifer looked at him...

"Dyna... whatever you said is true," he exclaimed.

Slowly, slowly his body started turning into ashes...he died...

"NO ...dad...don't go." Lucifers and Dyna mourning on his left ashes.

Marcus hugged Olivia and others ...a wave of happiness spread all over.

Richard and Henry overwhelmed with their victory, but something is still bothering them because they know it's not that easy to defeat Draco so sudden.

"He wasn't that fool," Henry said to Richard...Richard who was also quite confused and unsure about Draco's death he just nodded trying to calculate the reality of the fact.

"Apparently, he was week because of the killing spell, perhaps he withdrew his powers...or..."

"Something is fishy..., something is bothering me, I don't know but I couldn't feel the satisfaction in this victory," Henry said cutting him in between.

He worriedly looks around for any foul play..., "nothing suspicious Dad." Olivia chuckled hugging him.

"Amen," Henry said hugging her.

Every present wizard guest was celebrating the death of the cruel king Draco.

Giggles echoed suppressing Lucifer's mourn.

Dyna was drenched in tear looking at the giggling crowd.

"Stop laughing!" Lucifer's growled at the crowd.

CHAPTER-47 "DRACO IS BACK"

"STOP IT!"

"Lucifer's growled at the crowd.

Marcus and all others are busy celebrating their victory.

Suddenly his growling turned into a demonic laugh.

Everyone stopped giggling and was stunned to see Lucifer laughing.

People thought he lost his mental stability in shock.

Dyna devilishly smirking wiping her tears.

All of a sudden strong winds starting blowing, black clouds, darkening the ambience,

Everyone panicked, winds turned into storms getting stronger and stronger.

Everything started falling here and there, giggles turned into screams, people trembled couldn't able to balance falling on the floors.

Arthur and Zenia crawled to Henry to save him,

Marcus tightly held Richard preventing him to fall,

Olivia and Lily couldn't balance themselves and fall down from the huge stage.

Both got injured.

"Oliviaaa..." Marcus screamed.

A huge dark black cloud comes over the stage.

Lucifer's and Dyna's eyes glowered,

The black cloud slowly changed into a human figure in a black cloak, a loud demonic laughed echoed...

The figure fiercely landed on the stage, and the storm stops. Everyone tries to stabilise themselves, few are injured and looking for their loved ones.

Every guest drizzly trying to figure out the person behind the cloak.

The demonic laugh grew louder and louder.

The figure slowly shoved his cloak and every eye widened to see Draco.

People panicked to see Draco alive.

"Giggle now, celebrate your victory now...you cowards...you losers." Draco roared at the crowd,

"Hellooo… dear friends, I am so obliged to see my dearest friends happy and ALIVE standing in front of me." Draco sneered looking at Richard and Henry.

Arthur came in between them, to protect Henry,

Henry slightly pushed Arthur away to confront Draco.

"DAD…" Zenia muttered.

Henry winked at Zenia to calm her down,

Arthur held Zenia's hand tightly.

"Draco, your enmity is with me…let others go away," Henry groaned.

"No, my friend my enmity is never with you, unless you refused my proposal," Draco responded.

"I am not your friend!" Henry said gritting his teeth,

"Ohh, I remember you are indeed friends with Snake's king, you always admired this betrayer as your friend, "Draco growled pointing his wand towards Richard.

"Richie never betrayed." Henry bellowed scowls.

"He always betrayed, he betrayed me, he will betray you as well." Draco scoffed…

"I never betrayed anyone," Richard huffed.

"You did…, I WAS NEVER LIKE THIS, I was also a good boy it was you and you who forced me to turn evil, you fetched my love…It's you and only you Richard." Draco growled attacking Richard with his spell.

Richard grunts in pain.

Marcus frowned, his face turned red in anger, he tried to enchant a spell on Draco raising his wand, he tried again and again but his powers were not working.

Draco laughed looking at his powerless wand and useless efforts to attack him,

"You fool…" Draco attacked Marcus and he flew away with the flash of light and fall on the ground,

"Marcusss…," Arthur screamed.

"What you want Draco?" Zenia yelled…

"Oh, little girl, don't push yourself so hard," Lucifer said brushing his fingers over her arms.

"Stay away from her…" Arthur frowned shoving his hands away.

Zenia ran away to help Marcus to stand.

Draco looked down the stage at the panicked crowd,

"SOLDIERS… CAPTIVE THEM ALL…" he ruthlessly ordered.

The waiters who were courteously serving the guest an hour ago changed into dragon soldiers handcuffed all the guests with Draco's order.

"Nooo…" Henry groaned.

"Draco…, don't dig the graves of past…, your enmity is with us, let them go," Richard screamed.

"I am not digging the graves, Richie… it's you and only you who never let me heel." Draco groaned crouching near him.

"Stay away from dad." Arthur scowls.

As he was trying to move. Lucifer attacked him and grabbed Zenia's arms pulling her closer to him…

"Leave me…" Zenia screamed.

"Your beauty deserves a better man…someone like me, "Lucifer's smouldered sniffing her hair…

Arthur again tried to hit Lucifer, Dyna attacked him with a spell and Arthur flew away with a flash of light hitting him harder...

Arthur grunts in pain and smashed on a wall,

Marcus ran to Lucifers and clenched his throat…"You bastard…how dare you to touch her?"

Dyna immediately enchants a spell on Marcus throwing him away on the ground.

His wounds started bleeding more.

"Nooo…" Olivia screamed trying to get away from the grip of a soldier,

Dyna slowly walked to Marcus and leaned over him, who was trying to sit supporting his back on the wall,

"AAww love…why…why you force me to hurt you…? I can't see you hurt," Dyna shamelessly said wiping blood from the corner of his lips,

Marcus frowned shoving her hand away,

"You bitch…" he groaned,

"Come let me show you, love," Lucifer screamed trying to take Zenia away.

"Lucifer behave…, she is my friend's daughter." Draco stopped him.

"You will get enough time to love her later," he smirked.
Draco signalled the soldiers to captive all.

A soldier came closer to Marcus to arrest him.

Dyna stopped him showing him her hand.
He stopped.

"I will take him with me, he is my captive," she ordered.

"No, never, I never will go with you, you betrayer." He groaned.

"O really...I betrayed you, you can replace Olivia with me, and I even can't replace your wand...that's not fair love," she said mocking.

Soldiers pushing all captives towards the prison.

Draco laughed loudly looking at the panicked captives.

"DRACO IS BACK!" "DRACO IS BACK!"

Draco devilishly roared.

<u>CHAPTER-48 "GAME CHANGED"</u>

All the dragon soldiers were taking the captives to the prison and Draco, Lucifer was laughing looking at their miserable condition.

Dyna was about to take Marcus to her room,

Three lighting tornadoes appear on the stage randomly attacking the dragons with their spell, thousands of flashes of lighting, hitting and killing the dragons.

Draco and Lucifers frowned at the unexpected attack.

Lucifer's counter-attack at one of the tornados but his spell didn't work.

Dyna jerked with the attack, Marcus immediately snatched Dyna's wand and broke it into pieces.

All dragons soldiers started falling to the ground because of the powerful attack.

Draco panicked looking around his defeating army,

"Draco...YOUR GAME IS OVER."

A loud voice echoed.

One of the tornadoes changed to Queen Vincent while the other two tornadoes kept attacking the leftover dragons.

Before Draco and other dragons could stabilize.

Vincent throws the red wands towards Marcus and Arthur.

Arthur and Marcus successfully catch their powerful wands.

All dragons army vanished from the battlefield.

The other two tornadoes turned to Lord Reece and King Zohan respectively.

Lord Reece holding a huge crystal emitting a very bright light. as soon as the light falls on Draco.

Draco frowned...

"Lord..., No...NO... you can't do that to me..." He growled.

His growling didn't work.

"Vincent ..., why do you always refuse me? Why you stand against me. I loved you so much... and... I still love you the same way?" he groaned.

His powers getting demolished with the bright light.

"I never refused you Draco...I am against your evil practices and hatred that you have in your heart." She responded fiercely walking through.

"I turn evil because of your rejection, you chose Richard over me... even though I was more handsome, more powerful than him." he scoffs.

"Richard never killed any innocent...Draco" she responded shouting.

"You betrayed your wife...he never did anything like that to anyone that is why I chose him, loved him and married him...Draco...I feel pity for you." she said walking towards him.

He kneeled down because of the pain as all his energy withdrawn from his body,

"Father in law you too? You too are standing with my enemies. I couldn't move for 15 years because of them only. Rose your beloved daughter died of the trauma given by them." Draco saddens.

Arthur and Marcus enchant a spell on Lucifer and he freezes before Lucifer could attack them.

Olivia and Zenia handcuffed Dyna with a spell.

Everyone reached the centre of the huge stage,

"You can't kill me so easily." Draco roared smirking.

"I know." Vincent chuckled.

"Just to destroy your unwavering confidence we planned this. We already knew that the coronation ceremony is just a trap of yours to imprisoned all the free kings."

"Moreover...the day I got my conscious, I was also aware of your recovery."

"But one thing... that you forget was...the magical diamond crystal." She said raising her hand towards Lord Reece.

Lord Reece was holding the Diamond crystal.

"In your hatred, you forget how powerful I will be with my crystal powers...My FOUR CRYSTAL ARE WITH ME." She shouted crouching near him.

"Admit your sins Draco...It's your last chance." Zohan said interrupting.

"Nothing to admit..." Draco scoffs.

"DAD..." Dyna screamed.

Draco looked at her crying.

His heart ached with his daughter's painful groans.

He raised his eyes looking at the sky.

The dark clouds turned into a Carbon Black Crown.

Everyone was shocked to see the huge crown again.

"What the hell?" Arthur frowned.

Draco excitedly looked at the crown before he can enchant the spell.

With Vincent's signal...All the four crystals i.e., Arthur, Zenia, Marcus and Olivia raised their wands at the crown.

"Attack," Vincent ordered raising their wands in unison at the crown.

The rays of lighting from their wands and the crystal strikes the crown.

Crown burst with a loud blast...,

Draco started screaming.

"NO! NO...nooo..."

Draco slowly, slowly fades away and disappeared into fumes.

Zohan enchants a spell at Lucifer and Dyna.

"Grandpa," Dyna ran to him crying.

"They killed dad." she said sobbing.

Lucifer mourns, but unable to showcase his emotions fall on his knees.

"I warned you about the destruction...I tried hard to change your mindset, I failed dad. I failed...Dad..." He mourns loudly screaming and stomping his hand on the ground.

"What are you saying Lucifer?" Dyna furiously asked.

"Grandpa informed me everything, he always worked for our well being but I was the one who always refused to admit that, yes, I saw mom crying for dad, I saw her dying for dad and because of the dad."

"Because of dad, how?" Dyna arching her brows at him.

"Dad asked her to die at his place and she lent her life to him, as mom always love dad and wanted him to live longer. I witnessed her sacrifices." Lucifer said crying.

"Dad never valued her sacrifices, I tried hard to be good but it was dad who always wanted me to be his heir...heir to his black magical powers...

I thought it was mom asking me for that but later I realised mom never wished her children to be cruel, she wanted us to be kind and humble wizards just like Arthur and Marcus." he said looking at the twin princes.

"Lucifer..." Dyna cried hugging him tightly.

Lucifer wiped his tears and firmly stood back.

He stretched his arms and enchants a spell, in the fiction of the time the whole dragon kingdom demolished.

Dyna understood why he demolished the whole kingdom.

"I am proud of you brother. We can't live in a kingdom which was built over the graves of innocents."

Everyone disappeared and the huge stage turns into debris.

CHAPTER-49 "HAPPILY EVER AFTER"

All of them appeared in the water palace.

Everyone was happy and relaxed.

Lucifer was somehow sad, but later he also calms down.

Marcus, Arthur and Richard were injured in the war. Lord Reece healed their wounds with his magical spell powers.

Everyone freshens up.

Zohan called everyone for a small celebration and ordered his staff to start serving beverages and snacks to all of them. The situation changed from an intense situation to a beautiful peaceful family party.

Happy faces, giggles and celebrations.

"Mom, You did a fab job today!" Marcus said raising his wine glass.

"Thanks, son." She replied.

"Marcus, you should learn some lessons from this!" Vincent exclaimed.

"I mean, you shouldn't underestimate your enemies strength."

"Yes, mom, you said it right," Marcus said.

She continued "You didn't think about Plan B."

"Apparently Draco was ahead of you in his planning...he sniffed your strategy and planned meticulously."

"I already informed you how cruel he was, and you still thought you trounced him so easily.

You were overconfident at that time. But, I would like to tell all of you that, I was working on another plan with Lord Reece, Zohan and Olivia." Vincent said wrapping her arm around Olivia's shoulder.

"I must say Marcus...my daughter in law is more modest and intelligent than you." She chuckled grabbing Olivia's hand.

Olivia blushed with her words and Marcus look at Olivia smirking.

"I agree mom!" Arthur said in a teasing tone.

"When you all left for the ceremony. Olivia came to me, she was quite uncertain about your strategy. So we started working on our Plan B."

"We straight away reached Zohan and called Lord Reece for our help and the first thing that strikes our mind to defeat Draco is our crystal powers. We all went to the lake and activated the drowned magical crystal."

"Moreover, when I get to know, How Draco manipulatively wins over you all? We sent Olivia first just to know the criticality of the situation and when we lost the mind link with Olivia. I understood that Draco again played his dirty cards. We immediately planned to attack him with the crystal powers and rest is very well known to you all." she sighed.

"Let's forget it all! All well that ends well!" Zohan said cheering up everyone.

"Ladies and Gentlemen," Zohan loudly called for attention.

"I have an important announcement to make," he said smiling.

"Lucifer and Dyna come here," he called him close to him.

"It's time for my retirement now." He said with a 1000 watt smile.

"I king Zohan, king of the Kingdom of Sea, hereby announces my grandson Lucifer the New and Young King of the Kingdom of Sea."

Lucifers eyes widened in shock and Dyna and everyone applauded.

"Congrats bro." Dyna chuckled.

"I also love to announce, Dyna, My loving granddaughter the New and Beautiful heiress of the Kingdom of Whales."

Dyna's eyes watered hearing that she emotionally hugged him in surprise.

"I will never let you down grandpa," Lucifer promised him.

"I believe you son," he said wrapping his arms around him.

Everyone cheered toasting for them.

Everyone congratulates Lucifer and Dyna, Lord Reece blessed them.

"So, when are you getting married, my ultimate winners?" Reece asked Arthur and Marcus.

"Before that, there is something more important that needs to be done," Richard said interrupting and every eye curiously turned to Richard.

"Re-coronation of my best friend Henry," Richard said frothing towards Henry.

"Re coronation?" Henry surprisingly asked.

"Yes, my friend, I have already planned everything, your all-new Kingdom crystal and your lovely Crystal Palace is waiting for his King and Queen." He chuckled.

"What??" Lily's eyes moisten hearing that.

"Yes, Lily, tomorrow is the day of celebration...in fact double celebration," Vincent said.

"Wooow! I am stoaked, Richie. It will be the best gift of my life." Henry chuckled hugging his friend.

"Tomorrow, We will be going to announce your wedding as well." Lily chortled looking at her daughters.

Zenia and Olivia exchanged glances and shyly looked at their fiances.

The whole happy atmosphere.

The next morning everyone got busy looking around for arrangements for the re-coronation ceremony at the new Crystal Palace.

The shining glass crystal palace was majestic creation of the artists.

The Crystal Royal family came walking on the red carpet.

Lily in the white royal gown, silver crown sparkling over her head enhancing the shine of the ambience. King Henry in his white royal king suit.

Zenia and Olivia giving an angelic appearance in their lavender embellished gown.

The Smith family entered the celebrations, the twin princes wearing a black tuxedo and the King and queen wearing royal attires.

Lord Reece, Zohan, Lucifer and Dyna also came for the celebrations.

Grand ceremony, lots of guests, all happily enjoying the moment.

Henry and Lily walked to the huge stage.

Lord Reece already standing there waiting for them.

Henry and Lily greeted him.

Lord Reece happily coronated Henry with the Crystal Crown.

Henry later announced the engagement of Zenia with Arthur and Olivia with Marcus.

Both the couples exchanged engagement rings.

Everyone enjoyed the ceremony.

Richard and Vincent also get there to live back free in their Palace with family.

Jacob was sent to prison.

Arthur and Zenia get more time to know each other. Zenia loves to spend time with Arthur. She also helps him in his hospital. Both enjoy each others company.

Marcus kept asking for Olivia's forgiveness and she finally forgives him. Marcus also desired Olivia to join his business. Olivia happily accepted his proposal as she always wanted to be an independent working woman. She also generously donated a huge sum of money to the Pinewood Orphanage. Olivia finally has her parents and sister, the honour, the love, the respect, the picture of her dream family is now complete by the grace of God.

Marcus is also happy to have his parents healthy and safe staying together with him.

The perfect family Marcus and Olivia always wished to have are now complete.

Zenia also gets her sister back.

"I am so happy to have you Zen," Arthur said with sparkling eyes full of affection.

"I am also very happy." Zenia chuckled running her fingers in his hair.

He pulled her more closer to him, she shyly looks into his eyes and trail to the moments of love.

Marcus is happier as he finally gets the perfect moment he always waited to be with Olivia.

Olivia was in her room shyly smirking looking at the engagement ring she was wearing.

Preparations for their wedding were in full swing.

Zenia and Olivia are always busy in shopping. Arthur and Marcus often joined them in shopping or sometimes they both enjoy their sisterly time.

Arthur wants the ceremony to be simple whereas Zenia's want it to be a grand ceremony.

On the other hand, Marcus wants his wedding to be a classy ceremony and Olivia agreed with him, as nothing is more important for her than to be with her family and her love.

"Oliv...I don't like this." Marcus frowned while selecting their honeymoon destination.

"What...?" Olivia confusedly looks at him.

"I don't like you being submissive and obedient to me all the time. I want you to be stubborn sometimes, sometimes rebel, at least disobey me once or throw some wifey tantrums." he frowned.

Olivia laughed looking at her frowning fiance.

"Why are you laughing?" Marcus scoffs.

"Whatever you chose for me is the best, Marcus, then why I rebel?" she exclaimed wrapping her arms around his neck.

"I like to see you happy, your happiness is everything to me."

"You gave back my family to me, what else I can ask?" she said looking deep into his eyes.

"I love you," Olivia.

"I love you even more Marcus."

 A month later a grand wedding ceremony was held in the crystal palace.

Wizards from the whole magical world were invited.,

Crystal Palace was shining brightly under the decorative lights and lamps.

Olivia and Zenia were looking stunning in their white bridal gowns and the grooms look handsome in their dark brown tuxedos.

Both the couples took their wedding vows and once again they sealed their love when the priest pronounced them Husband and Wife.

They all live HAPPILY EVER AFTER.

THANK YOU

Regards,
Unité Publication
Stay Connected!